"Just what are you asking me to do, Cade?"

Maureen asked, drawing away from him.

"I'll rephrase my offer, Maureen. If you want me to help you out, I expect *you* to help *me* out."

Under normal circumstances, Maureen could have gathered her purse and pride and made a run for it, but these were not normal circumstances. She was there for a purpose.

"I might be willing to agree," she allowed.

His chuckle was low, harsh. "Then we have a deal." His heated gaze melted into the blue of hers. "How far are you willing to go?"

Reading lascivious intent, Maureen was halfway to the door before saying, "I'm not for sale or hire!"

Cade took Maureen's hand. "Why don't we back up a bit? My intentions weren't to hurt your feelings. Now, all you have to do is donate a couple of months of your time. In the role of my fiancée."

For once, Maureen was speechless.

Dear Reader:

Welcome to Silhouette Romance—experience the magic of the wonderful world where two people fall in love. Meet heroines who will make you cheer for their happiness and heroes (be they the boy next door or a handsome, mysterious stranger) who will win your heart. Silhouette Romance novels reflect the magic of love—sweeping you away with stories that will make you laugh and cry; heartwarming, poignant stories that will move you time and time again.

In the next few months, we're publishing romances by many of your all-time favorites such as Diana Palmer, Brittany Young, Annette Broadrick and many others. Your response to these authors and other authors in Silhouette Romance has served as a touchstone for us, and we're pleased to bring you more books with Silhouette's distinctive medley of charm, wit and—above all—*romance*.

During 1991, we have many special events planned. Don't miss our WRITTEN IN THE STARS series. Each month in 1991, we're proud to present readers with a book that focuses on the hero—and his astrological sign.

I hope you'll enjoy this book and all of the stories to come. Come home to romance—Silhouette Romance—for always!

Sincerely,

Tara Gavin
Senior Editor

MARTHA HIX

Texas Tycoon

Silhouette *Romance*

Published by Silhouette Books New York

America's Publisher of Contemporary Romance

SILHOUETTE BOOKS
300 E. 42nd St., New York, N.Y. 10017

TEXAS TYCOON

ISBN: 0-373-08779-9

First Silhouette Books printing March 1991

Printed in the U.S.A.

Books by Martha Hix

Silhouette Special Edition
Every Moment Counts #344

Silhouette Romance
Texas Tycoon #779

MARTHA HIX

is the mother of two grown daughters and lives in San Antonio, Texas, with her husband and a menagerie of pets. When she's not busy writing, she enjoys outdoor activities and researching genealogy. What doesn't she like? Dieting and housework.

NEW MEXICO

Amarillo

OKLAHOMA

ARKANSAS

TEXAS

Dallas

Midland

LOUISIANA

Austin

Dry Hole Ranch

Houston

San Antonio

N

MEXICO

Gulf of Mexico

Underlined places are fictitious.

Chapter One

She hated what was going on. It wasn't that Maureen Miniver was behind schedule in baking forty dozen Granny Miniver's Famous chocolate-chip cookies, or that the ancient oven in her inadequate kitchen was on its last legs, or even that she was down to her last shekels. While these problems caused an inordinate amount of concern during the daily operation of her cookie factory, Maureen had a bigger problem: her live-in stepfather and his wayward son.

"Sugar Pie, are you listening to me?" Wilburn Herrington asked. A grin split his handsome and aged face as he stopped chopping pecans to hold aloft the business section of the San Antonio *Express-News*. "What a way to start the morning. That boy of mine has done it again. He's a rich one, yes he is."

The cookie batter received a rough stir. "I'm pleased for Cade," Maureen said, but the words were a bold-faced lie spoken in her adored stepfather's best interest. In truth, she resented Cade Herrington's hard-hearted nature.

But her mother's widower was proud of his only son's accomplishments, and loved him unequivocally, even though Cade had chosen to distance himself from his father. Exactly why, she didn't know, despite her many questions over the years. Three months ago, when Wilburn arrived on the doorstep of the modest rented house that also served as bakery headquarters, Maureen had become even more aware of his overpowering need to be a part of his son's life. She doubted that would ever happen.

Wilburn, his eyes downcast, refolded the newspaper. "I used to be like him. 'Course, I'm not rich now. But I will be again. Someday. Soon as I get a foot in the door."

Feeling a tug of love and sympathy, she said, "Keep the spirit. Success starts with a dream. And I admire yours."

"And I admire your entrepreneur's spirit. Someday this bakery is going to make you a rich woman."

The yen to be wealthy wasn't a big thing, but she did strive for solid ground with her three-year-old cookie factory. "I must admit . . . having the money to operate properly would be nice. More than nice."

"Just need a bit of luck, that's all. It's about time you and me had some, too. Like I had with Pemberton Couplings. Why, I put that outfit into shape in no time, and we were in the black—" he snapped his fingers "—quick as that."

Maureen, her hand in a disposable glove, spooned dough onto a baking sheet. She had heard his story over and over. Pemberton Couplings had belonged to his first wife, Rowena—Cade's mother. The company had been on the brink of financial disaster when Wilburn took over to make it a success. Then he was forced out by divorce, twenty years ago.

After that, the pettish cycles of the petroleum industry had worked against him, as they had for many, many others. Each time he had gotten the funds to open a new oil-service company, the price of West Texas crude plummeted. During such downturns, few operators had a need for drill-pipe fittings; it wasn't economically feasible to explore for black gold, unless one had the time and money to speculate or to court OPEC. Of course, there was always the lucky oilman who rode shotgun with good fortune. Cade Herrington, the ingrate son, was such a man.

She slapped the oven door closed, wishing she could slam a door on the man who had broken his father's heart.

"Have I upset you, Sugar Pie? Didn't mean to."

"Oh, hush, you. You don't upset me."

"But have I told you lately how much I appreciate your taking me in after I went broke this last time?" Wilburn asked.

She set a tray of cookies on the cooling rack and squeezed his blue-veined hand. "Thanks aren't needed."

Gratitude was a two-way street. Before Doris Miniver had married Wilburn, no one had had the time to make Maureen feel loved, since her father died when she was a toddler and her mother had struggled in her widowhood to put food on the table. Then Wilburn came along, when Maureen was twelve, not only to give his second wife a helping hand but also to shower love on the ready-made family. He was the father Maureen had yearned for. And their relationship had grown even stronger in the three years since Doris's death.

Wilburn grinned. "Such a pretty gal you are. Those eyes—mmm, mmm! Why, they're as blue as sapphires and as full of lights as diamonds on a rich widow's pinkie. They'd turn any man to mush. And that sable hair. Even when it's all squashed under a hair net, it shines with life."

"You're embarrassing me. Stop that silly talk."

Naturally he didn't. The callused thumb that had held a pencil, years back, to assist Maureen with her homework and had wiped away her tears on many occasions, touched her jaw. "Never knew a woman as pretty on the inside as she was on the outside, 'cept for you and your mama. It's a shame some rich man doesn't take you out of this kitchen."

"Yes, and it's a shame pigs can't fly." Two cooled cookies, both wafting the aromas of chocolate, pecans, sugar and vanilla, were plucked from a box to wave under his nose. "How about breakfast? That ought to stop the philosophizing."

"Aw now." Wilburn winked a right eye. "I love you, you know. You're a good girl."

Maureen sighed. Nearing twenty-four and with a heavy load of responsibilities, she felt anything but a girl.

Not prone to letting any point go, Wilburn added, "You deserve better than you've got, but we won't be paupers forever, Maureen." He used her given name only when most sincere. "We need a grubstake, that's all. And I've got an idea rolling around upstairs." Stressing his last words, he tapped his head. "Like I always say, it takes money to make money."

"I agree."

Wilburn grew pensive. "Speaking of success, think I'll send my boy one of those congratulatory telegrams."

Words about saving effort and money died in Maureen's throat. "That's a great idea. I'm sure he'll appreciate it." She turned to the oscillating fan, letting the breeze cool her face. June in Texas was hotter than a jalapeño pepper on an uninitiated tongue, and the air conditioner was no match for the heat radiating from the oven. "But don't get in a black funk this time if you don't hear from him."

"I won't. I know Cade's a busy man."

Anger burned through Maureen. A month ago she had telephoned Cade at his penthouse in the Fortuna Building, but he had been short with her, saying he was late for an engagement. After that, the telephone number was changed to unlisted status. When she rang his office, she got the runaround. "He isn't taking any calls" or "He's at his ranch, and I can't give out the unlisted number" had translated to "He doesn't want to see his father."

If only Cade would give him half a chance....

Wilburn creased the newspaper. "I worry about him. He needs to get himself a family and quit devoting himself to high-flying bachelor ways. I've read the gossip columns. He's always got this or that gorgeous gal on his arm, but he never stays with one of them for long." He grimaced. "He hasn't learned the lesson I learned the hard way. A happy marriage makes a difference in a man's life."

Though Wilburn was open and frank, he rarely spoke of his marital problems with Cade's mother, but Maureen was aware that the bitter and resentful Rowena Pemberton Herrington had refused, post divorce, to allow fatherly visitation rights. And three years later, upon reaching his eighteenth birthday, Cade had declined to start visiting on his own.

Why was Cade so heartless? She knew for a fact that Wilburn had made every effort to show his love, and that he didn't understand his son's attitude, either, even though he was quick to make excuses.

"Yep. I'll bet he's lonesome as a polecat at a Sunday picnic." Wilburn's tone didn't match his attempt at humor.

"Now don't jump to conclusions. He's got his work and his ranch. I imagine he stays plenty busy."

"Holing up in some weekend retreat doesn't compare to married life." Wilburn nudged the newspaper in Maureen's direction. "It's not his looks keeping him from the altar."

She studied the picture smiling up from the article. Like his father in his younger days, Cade Herrington was black-haired, square-jawed and handsome in the way that attracted women. But not Maureen. Not anymore.

She recalled their last face-to-face, six years ago. Wilburn had insisted on driving to San Antonio from Midland to "put a present under my boy's tree"; they had arrived at Cade's penthouse on Christmas Eve. *That time* he hadn't shown them the door, had gone so far as to offer cups of eggnog. In the season's spirit?

As she'd sipped her drink, Maureen had stared at Cade, thinking he had an interesting quality. He was unattainable, out of reach. A challenge.

Back then, she'd thought such a trait appealing, but her assessment had changed when Cade returned Wilburn's modest gift. Unopened. Doris—hoping to spare her dear husband's feelings—had thrown the handmade tie rack in the trash bin, but Wilburn had found it. It was one of the two times Maureen had seen him cry. From that day on, she'd disliked Cade Herrington.

Maureen's thoughts were cut off by a series of knocks on the ancient front door. No one was expected, since her right-hand woman, Janece Stewart, was making deliveries. A mischievous grin lifted the gulleys of Wilburn's face.

Good-naturedly she asked, "All right. What's up?"

"Get the door, and you'll find out."

She did, and nothing in her wildest imagination could have prepared her for the shock she received.

Twenty minutes later the deliverymen departed, leaving a crate in the kitchen corner. With receipt in hand, Maureen faced the culprit. "How could you?"

"We needed a new stove, so I bought us one."

"On credit." A sick feeling lurched in her stomach.

"Don't worry about a thing." Wilburn rifled through the toolbox for installation supplies. "We'll pay for this new beauty. It's just a pittance a month."

"For the next—" She glanced at the ticket, her eyes growing round. "For the next three years."

Right then, the old oven door flapped open like a giant protruding tongue to add to Wilburn's case. Maureen groaned with disgust before kicking the oven closed.

"Settle down." Wilburn's hand shot up to pat the air. "I've got an idea.... We can make big bucks, and this new industrial oven will help us along."

We. Us. Biting her tongue to keep from reminding him that Granny Miniver's Famous was her company, she forced patience. "Does this idea have anything to do with the 'upstairs' idea you mentioned earlier?"

"It does." He tossed a roll of electrical tape on the counter. "We'll bake a batch of those chocolate-chip wonders, and I'll carry them up to Dallas. To Texas Bakeries."

Just as she suspected, Wilburn Herrington had set his mind on being a part of her dream, not on plans of his own. That was the crux of the problem.

Delivery ticket tucked beneath the utility bill and a host of other payables, she asked, "What would the state's largest commercial bakery want with my baked goods?"

"To package them, of course. We're going to sell the licensing rights to Granny Miniver's Famous."

"I'll have no part of that."

"I think you will. You've got recipes just as good and, if not better than the chocolate-chip one, and when they buy the rights to your name, we'll have freedom to explore new avenues. As soon as they buy us out, we'll lasso that old gristmill you've had your eye on."

Money worries relegated to a corner of her mind, Maureen reverted to a dream she had held for three years. Turning Cutter's Mill into a bakery. Picturesque and unique, the old gristmill, which had been built by German settlers in the nineteenth century, hugged a bend in Cibolo Creek between San Antonio and New Braunfels. A lot of work and money would be involved in converting the building into a

commercial bakery, but the mill was a treasure. If only...
If, if, if!

If there was ever a moment for honesty, this was it. "I
don't want to hurt your feelings, but I make the decisions
where business is concerned."

"Are you saying you don't want me as a partner?"

"I want you to do what's best for you, not me. Your place
is not in a kitchen, it's outdoors, doing what you do best.
You've had forty years of experience in the oil field, and you
need to get back to it."

"I see." The spark left his brown eyes; his shoulders
sagged. "I never thought it would come to this. But I guess
it's to be expected. You young folks deserve the chance to
make it on your own. And you're right. I should butt out.
Look how well Cade's done without my interference."

She had hurt him, and she moved to hug his pain away.
"I'm sorry," she whispered. "I'm not turning my back on
you. I would never do that."

As she spoke, an idea formed in Maureen's head. Should
she tell Wilburn? Not yet. Not until she had positive results. After all, her plan—involving Cade in Wilburn's financial affairs to restore father-son bonding—wasn't
foolproof, but she figured there was nothing to lose and
maybe everything to gain.

Yes, Maureen thought, she had to give it a try. Because
Wilburn needed her help.

Cade Herrington needed help.

A Bloody Mary would be a good start, he decided and
paced his luxurious office overlooking the San Antonio
River Walk. As he fought to give attention to his business
partner and mentor, Cade was nursing the worst hangover
of his life.

"You look more like forty-five than almost thirty-five, and you truly look like hell," Douglas Smythe commented, bracing an ankle over an expensively clad knee. "That daughter of mine must've put you through the wringer last night."

"No comment."

Sandra Smythe Uhr was indeed the cause of Cade's temporary illness, brought on by imbibing too much of her sugary Asti Spumante and searching for a way to let her down easily.

"Sandra thinks you're ready to pop the question," Douglas said, fishing.

Cade winced. If there was anything he was positive about, beyond his dedication to attaining the presidency of Petroleum Producers Association in August, it was that Sandra wanted to become Mrs. Cade Herrington.

After separating from her husband, she had decided fate brought Cade her way, and that he was going to be her next husband. She expected as much. Everything came easily to her; he had never known her to set her sights on something and work to get it.

She'd miss her target where Cade was concerned. His feelings were brotherly, and the fireworks just weren't there. That was the way he liked his women—the Fourth of July, exploding in fiery flashes never to be seen again.

Temporary women, the challenges of plumbing oil from the ungiving earth and the spoils of wealth were de rigueur for Cade. Yet his hard-won riches afforded him a diversion from the fast lane: the quiet of his hill-country ranch. Under the open skies, he relaxed. Yep, he congratulated himself, he had a good life. If he could get that PPA presidency and could get Sandra off his back, everything would be dandy.

"Cade? Is there any truth to the rumor?"

He needed an out, and he needed it badly. "That's between me and Sandra," Cade hedged.

"You're right." Douglas sighed. "But don't forget. Marriage would help your case with the conservative PPA membership. They'll never elect you as president as long as Jake Patton keeps reminding them of your marital status."

The hangover got worse. Winning that presidency was a longtime goal of Cade's, and he'd do *anything* to get it.

"Sit down, for heaven's sake, Cade, so we can get back to the business at hand. That's better."

Cade picked up the prospectus on a newly purchased piece of property. "About the Cutter's Mill tract, the surveys look promising for exploration. We—"

His secretary interrupted, opening the door between her office and Cade's. "Excuse me, gentlemen."

"What's the problem?"

"It's...it's—" Gloria Guerra glanced imploringly at her employer "—it's Ms. Miniver. The lobby guard says she's on her way up here."

Cade clenched his fist. To this point, he had been able to evade the recent telephone campaign of Wilburn Herrington and Maureen Miniver. Why couldn't they get the picture? He neither wanted nor needed his father in his life, and hadn't for a long time—not since Wilburn, his fingers clamped around Pemberton money, had broken his mother's heart.

Never once during the fifteen remaining years of her life had she heard as much as a whisper of regret or remorse from the old goat.

And now he had sent a messenger. "Get rid of her."

The secretary opened her mouth, but Cade cut in. "Tell her I'm at lunch. And by the way, order some. I don't care what, as long as it includes a Bloody Mary." He was talking fast. "I'll take it here. Join me, Doug?"

His lined face rife with question, Douglas shook his head. "Close the door behind you." When Gloria had complied, Cade said, "Doug, about Cutter's Mill—"

"Who's Ms. Miniver?" Douglas reached for a cigar and took a long time lighting it.

His mentor wasn't aware of the family connection, Cade knew, and now wasn't the forum for explanations. Although he had been aboveboard personally and professionally with Douglas, he didn't wish to involve him in this one particular problem. "She's a business associate."

"You don't neglect business associates."

"I'm making an exception."

Suddenly, the office door burst open as a tall and shapely brunet charged into the office, fire shooting from the lapis lazuli of her eyes. Maureen Miniver had arrived.

Cade's collar got tight. And hot.

"This is just as I thought," she said. "Lunch, my eye. You're avoiding me, Cade Herrington, and I won't stand for it!"

"I couldn't stop her." Behind Maureen, the secretary waved her hand in a frantic motion of helplessness.

"I'll handle it, Ms. Guerra. Go back to your desk." Aggravated at the intrusion, at the gall of the intruder, Cade leaned back and made an effort to ignore the arresting difference six years had made in Maureen's appearance. "Ms. Miniver, as you can see, I'm in conference right now."

"*Ms.* Miniver? Why the new formality?"

Why, indeed. Tension crackled through Cade's veins, arcing across the ten feet separating him from Wilburn's advocate. After what that old no-account had done to Cade's now-deceased mother, he wanted no reminders that his father even existed.

Measuring his tone, Cade requested, "Please wait outside, Maureen."

"No way." She planted her slender feet firmly to the carpet and folded her arms. "You've been avoiding me, and I want to know why."

Every muscle in his six-foot-one body tight as a spring, Cade turned to Douglas, who had disapproval written all over his features. "Let me get back with you."

"That seems in order." The older man rose to his feet, giving Maureen a comforting smile. "Excuse me," he said more to her than to Cade as he exited.

"Sit down, Maureen."

He watched her move, and her motions were graceful. Cade was aggravated but he wasn't immune to her looks and style. He had tried not to notice those attributes in the past—how old was she then? Seventeen? Eighteen? Whatever. She was no longer a girl.

Seated in the chair Douglas had abandoned, she slid one shapely ankle across the other. "Cade, your father needs you."

"Is he sick or dying?"

"No." She eyed him squarely. "Would it make any difference if he were?"

"No."

"Why? Why isn't your father important to you? What happened between the two of you to cause such a rift?"

He refused to answer, but did study her blue, blue eyes. Eyes said a lot about a person. And hers? There was anger in and behind them. Which wasn't his problem. "I don't owe you an explanation."

"Maybe not. But your father's got one coming. He's at a time when he needs you the most. He'll be sixty-five on his next birthday, yet you ignore him, and that's unpardonable. He's never done anything but love you, while you . . . you treat him as if he were poison."

Apparently, she didn't know the ugly truth about Wilburn Herrington's philandering or about how easily he'd sell his soul. Cade wasn't going to set her straight, and being honest with himself, he realized he couldn't. Some things, some hurts, were too raw to verbalize.

Wilburn Herrington was not a father to be proud of.

"So, the old man sent you to rap my knuckles," Cade said, his head pounding from the aftermath of alcohol and the present subject matter. "Right?"

"I'm here of my own accord."

Why was that? Or was she? He studied his stepsister as she brushed a stray lock of shoulder-length sable hair behind her ear. Despite himself, he noticed the beautiful sheen and vibrancy of those thick, wavy tresses. Hell, she was beautiful, period. But he shouldn't allow himself to be attracted to anything about Maureen Miniver. She was too close to Wilburn Herrington. Too close for comfort. Off limits.

It took all of Cade's strength of conviction not to give in to temptation, though, and let down his guard.

He managed to stand, rest his palms on the desktop and ask, "What exactly do you want?"

"For you to spend some time with your father."

"Is that all?" he asked. "No, thanks."

"He could use your financial help, too."

I should've known. "Sorry again," Cade replied with forced detachment. "Time is precious, and I don't squander my money on lost causes."

"You dislike him because he's had financial setbacks? You're a mean man, Cade."

"You're right on the last point, wrong on the first. I've been around the oil patch long enough to realize anyone can fall victim to finances."

"But you've never known hard times. You got rich during the last oil boom and never hit a dry hole, didn't you? You've gotten even richer during the downturn." Her throaty voice rose in pitch. "Must be heady stuff, being a millionaire at twenty-four, and now ten years later, well..."

"... my millions are counted in the hundreds. But my financial status has nothing to do with the problem. I dislike him because he's a dreamer." Okay, he was skating over the truth. So what? "The way I figure it, a person either does or he doesn't. I does—he doesn't. It's as simple as that."

"He can and will if you'll give him a chance. Lend him some money. Fifty thousand ought to be enough. And let him know you're doing it, so he'll think you care for him."

"I don't care what he thinks."

"Please, Cade. Please reconsider. I'll stand good for the money. With, um, interest of course."

No one with good business sense put that much on the line for an old man who would beat her out of the money, either by greed or ineptitude or both. Wondering if she was stupid or simply bluffing, Cade decided on the latter. "What's in it for you?"

Her determined chin hitched an inch higher, as she replied, "The satisfaction of your father's happiness."

"I'll bet. I'd also bet he's promised you something in return for digging money out of me."

"Untrue."

Cade picked up his gold pen and studied the barrel. "I wouldn't wager on that."

Life had convinced him that everyone was out for *numero uno,* and that anything or anyone could be bought if the stakes were high enough. No doubt she figured to gain something.

Cade called her bluff. "Fifty thou plus interest means you'd have to sell a lot of cookies by the loan's due date."

Her eyes rounded. "You know about my cookie factory?"

"Know about the independent young woman who masquerades as a sweet little old grandma baking cookies out of her cozy kitchen? Yes, I know about her." Being a devotee of the *Express-News's* financial pages, he was up on local business. Recently, the newspaper had run an article about Maureen, and he'd been duly impressed, despite himself. The bakery put out an excellent product and was well-known in South Texas, the column had mentioned, and Granny Miniver's Famous had a faithful clientele. Cade was well aware of the product's quality. "Actually, I'm a customer."

Her obvious amazement manifested itself in an unintelligible stammer, and Cade drew a conclusion. Maureen Miniver wasn't as confident of herself as she should be.

"You have every reason to be proud of your success," he commented.

"I . . . I've worked hard at it, but . . . well, my cookie factory is small stuff compared to Fortuna Enterprises."

"You've made something out of nothing. That's to be admired."

Cade caught the twinkle that lit her blue eyes. He could feel his grin widen, and realizing how warm he was to her vulnerability, he checked his impulses. Better to cut the meeting short and get back to work. Or to the Bloody Mary, which was beginning to sound better and better.

Easing his shoulders against the high-back executive chair, Cade made his words cool. "It's been nice chatting with you, but I'm busy, so you can see your way out."

"Are you telling me no?"

"Exactly. I'll never cough up a big wad of dough for Wilburn Herrington."

"Never say never." Leaning forward, Maureen tapped an index finger against her bottom teeth before pointing at him. "Because you will help him. I'll see that you do."

"Is that a threat?"

"It's a promise, Cade Herrington. I've never backed down from a dare, and I don't intend to start with you."

"I don't doubt that for a moment," he said honestly and with admiration he hoped wasn't showing. Maureen was a woman of fire. His type of woman. He was close to surrender, but the voice of reason reminded him about her purpose. And there was the matter of the source of those demands.

"Save your energy," he said. "I bat a thousand in the big leagues. And if you're not careful, you'll get whopped by a homer past third base. Understand?"

Her oval face set. "You don't scare me."

"Maureen Miniver, you've got to the count of three to get out of here before I forcibly evict you."

"Save the strong-man tactics." She stood. "Rest assured, I haven't given up, but I will leave for now, Cad—oh my goodness!—I mean *Cade*."

With that she whirled around and stomped away.

He chuckled. Okay, she probably had ulterior motives, but unlike Sandra, Maureen fought for what she thought right. She was one helluva woman. Looks, fire, determination, vulnerability—she had them all. Provided he could keep Wilburn out of the picture, it would be worth fifty thousand dollars to have the pleasure of her company. *Yeah, and you just sent her away.*

He had another word with himself. Beyond his aversion to doing anything for his sire, Cade didn't have time for cat-and-mouse with his lovely stepsister. There was the Sandra problem; he had to find a solution that would keep their friendship intact. There was the PPA election. With Jake Patton as adversary, Cade had his work cut out for him.

He needed some neat little solutions to his problems. A neat, tidy resolution. One came to mind, but he dismissed it. But then again . . .

Not a man to leave anything to chance—wanting all the home runs off his bat—Cade picked up the telephone and dialed a number.

Chapter Two

From the fiasco of meeting with Cade, Maureen wasn't in the best of moods, and her frame of mind didn't improve overnight, or over the next one. She'd made a mess of things. It had been as plain as vanilla pudding that Cade hadn't appreciated her brand of hot-pepper demands. Flattery might have been a better tack. Her mother used to advise, "Lift a man's ego and he'll boost you up a pedestal." Sweet-talking obstinate men wasn't part of Maureen Miniver's repertoire.

But she had not quit the fight. Her next step? At this point on Sunday afternoon, no decision was firm. Early that day, Maureen had packed a solo picnic and had driven to Cutter's Mill. She did her best thinking on the banks of Cibolo Creek, in the shadow of her dreams.

Yet now, while she sat in the shade of a huge pecan tree, her knees tucked under her chin, the gristmill to her right, Maureen had a hard time concentrating on strategy.

Water tinkling over the crooked creek's sun-bleached rocks had a calming effect, though. The scent of loam and cropped grass filled her nostrils. Birds were singing. She glanced at the sky. A few clouds had formed, hinting at rain, yet it was a lovely day for shorts and halter tops and outdoors. It was a lovely day to sort out her next step with Cade.

Her thoughts took a different direction as her eyes settled on the gristmill. Two floors in height, the lovely old building was built in a blocky shape of limestone and now-weathered cedar. Window were broken, doors sagged on their hinges and a neck of the creek ran across the mill wheel's rotten planks. Maureen smiled. Cutter's Mill was the epitome of beautiful decay needing a loving heart's restoration.

She envisioned sparkling windows and fresh paint, newly cut boards rejuvenating the mill wheel to grind whole wheat for her recipes, plus an old-fashioned sign reading GRANNY MINIVER'S FAMOUS. But most of all, she foresaw a lovely working environment for herself and for her employees—lots of employees.

"And just where are you going to get the money for all that?" she muttered.

There was Wilburn's idea.... Selling out to Texas Bakeries didn't sit well with Maureen, though. She'd worked hard to establish the Granny Miniver name, and relinquishing it was akin to giving up a part of her pride. Besides, it was doubtful Texas Bakeries would be interested in buying her out. Wilburn's grandiose ideas were just that—grandiose.

From her basket, she retrieved a piece of fruit and a granola bar as a car pulled to a stop on the gravel road. Maureen swallowed a second bite of the red apple before paying mind to the intrusion or to the woman calling, "Hi, there."

Maureen wiped her mouth with a paper napkin and turned to the approaching stranger, a petite blonde who appeared to be in her early twenties. She wore an expensive Guatemalan peasant dress and oversize sunglasses, and her look was casual yet hoity-toity—the Alamo Heights type.

"Hello, yourself," Maureen returned, waving.

"I'm waiting for someone. Mind if I join you?"

"By all means, make yourself at home. Care for an apple?"

"No, thanks." The newcomer settled down in the St. Augustine grass, arranging her trim legs beneath her. A diamond pendant shaped as an *S* winked in the muted sunlight. "Have you seen a man wandering around here?"

"Sorry, no." Maureen raised a brow. "Peculiar spot to be meeting someone, out in the middle of nowhere."

"Not really. My boyfriend recently bought this place, and he's wanting to give it a look-see, so I offered to keep him company. Figured I'd get a late lunch out of the deal."

Some man had bought Cutter's Mill! Maureen's stomach knotted. Her eyes burned with tears she refused to shed. She hadn't expected the gristmill to stay on the market forever, but it had been vacant for years. Years!

Of course, the mill was merely a building and certainly not the last one on earth, but through her many struggles for solid footing with the cookie factory, she had banked on this place. None else would do.

She was shaking. But dreams die hard. And Maureen wasn't a woman to accept failure, once the initial shock had passed. Just because the gristmill had been sold didn't mean it wouldn't go on the market sometime in the future.

She pulled herself together. "Do you know what he plans to do with it?"

The Dresden doll of a girl brushed a speck of dirt from her shin and shrugged a shoulder. "I'm interested in the man, not in the toys he chooses to buy."

Maureen swallowed. So he looked on it as a toy, did he? Well, people had a way of tiring of playthings. All she had to do was bide her time—make some money—and she'd show him the difference between toys and serious business.

In the meantime, Maureen was well aware of one rule of business: Don't give the opponent an advantage. If she asked too many questions, the mystery man might get a report from this mystery woman. If he thought a buyer was interested, he'd add a zero or two to the selling price.

In the words of Muhammad Ali, she was going to float like a butterfly and sting like a bee.

Extremely pleased with herself for shoring up her dream, Maureen smirked. "Interested in the man, eh?"

A dulcet hum rolled from the girl. "Oh...yes." Her coral-glossed lips brightened into a smile. "He's a *dreamboat*. You know how that goes."

"Do I ever. But, darn, I just never have enough time for my dreamboat," she fabricated facetiously. In fact, she hadn't had a steady fellow in ages. Parroting her companion's words, she said, "You know how that goes."

"Not really. Why don't you tell me about it?"

Solemn now, Maureen eyed the mill. "I don't have many free hours, not with working six days a week."

"I'd never give so much of myself to some little job."

"I don't have a little job. I have my own business."

"That makes a difference, I'd imagine."

"You don't work?" Maureen asked, bemused.

"God, no. That's what men are for. As in Poppy and Hubby. Ex-hubby now."

Maureen pitied the stranger's lack of positive direction, and for some reason she had a ripe case of nosiness. "You don't work, you don't need money and you're divorced. So tell me, what do you do with your spare time?''

"Depends on the season. Autumns, I spend in Maine, winters in Aspen or Gstaad. In between, I do New York and London and Paris. Right now I should be in Ibiza, but I'm in the middle of a... Well, never mind."

Life for Maureen was cookies and dirty pans. She accepted that, because they financed, debatably, her independence. She loved the satisfaction of being her own boss, yet... she was a tad envious of the girl's freedom from responsibilities. "Your life sounds exciting."

"Not exactly." The young woman broke a blade of grass before tossing it away. Not another whisper passed her lips, and in that eloquent silence Maureen felt pity. Wealth hadn't brought the girl the happiness and excitement a poor woman would imagine came with the territory.

Feeling awkward, Maureen said the first thing that came to mind. "Tell me about the guy you're waiting for."

"He's my next husband."

"So, you're engaged?"

"Not yet. But soon."

"Expecting the big question any day now, then?"

"Any day."

"I see." But she didn't. Experienced in love and life, Maureen wasn't. Nonetheless, she had been around enough to know that the other woman's tone hadn't been working alive with the emotion one should have when speaking about a life mate. "Love him a lot, do you?" she goaded.

"In a... in a way. N-not in the same way I love—I mean, loved—my husband, but that doesn't stop me from wanting the marriage. It's the right thing to do. My father thinks we'd make a perfect couple. Besides, he's wonderful, and I—" The confessor sighed. "Gosh, you must think I'm crazy, spilling my guts to a stranger."

"Not at all. It's easier with someone you don't know, and will never see again." Right then a droplet of rain landed on Maureen's knee. "Shall we retire to the gristmill?"

"Hmm." The blonde glanced at the thin gold watch gracing her tiny-boned wrist. "Apparently, something's detained my boyfriend, so I'd better run along." She stood and fluttered her fingers. "I've enjoyed our little chat. Good luck to you and your business. Ciao." She strolled away.

Maureen got to her feet, then watched the girl's expensive white sports car spit gravel as it headed toward I-35. Maureen shook her head. She suspected the woman still loved her ex-husband. Her voice had had a catch in it when she'd mentioned him, and hadn't she tripped over the tense of love?

"Poor little rich girl."

Settled in her decrepit delivery van, Maureen engaged the windshield wipers and wondered if anyone ever got what they wanted in life. No doubt Cade did. Well, he didn't want Wilburn crowding his space—but that would change as soon as she devised a plan to lure him into being a proper son.

Maureen snapped her fingers as a strategy popped into her head. Any businesswoman who could sell cookies to bakeries ought to be able to sell a son on his father. Such a commercial approach was in order. Before, she had stressed what was in it for Wilburn, but on this go around, she intended to sell Cade on what was in it for him.

That in mind, she returned to San Antonio for a shower and change of clothes. Then, backtracking up I-35, she headed for Cade's ranch.

Maureen hadn't counted on an electric gate barring her from the Dry Hole Ranch. All wasn't lost, though. She spied a telephone-type intercom situated on one of the brick fence posts that guarded the ranch from outsiders.

Determination to sway the contrary millionaire toward being a good son propelled her to that telephone. She waited through ten rings. Cade wasn't expecting her, but she hadn't counted on the possibility he might not be on the premises. The half-hour trip northeast from the Alamo city to the New Braunfels area had been for naught.

"Blast it." She was on the verge of hanging up.

"Yeah?"

Her ear clip went flying as she yanked the receiver back. "Cade?" Static cut through the lines. "Is that you?"

A long pause. "What's up, Sandra?"

"I'm not Sandra." Whoever she was. "This is Maureen Miniver." Only the sound of a bad connection filtered through the line. "May I please have a minute of your time?" She crossed her fingers. "I promise it's to your advantage."

She heard a muttered "damn" before he replied, "Punch 3-6-7. We're at the main house. Follow the paving to the top of the hill."

The phone went dead.

Receiver and earring replaced, she wondered if he had a woman with him. No doubt one of his stable of lovelies. Well, she supposed Cade should be pleased that Sandra had not arrived to break up the cozy scene.

After giving her van a third turn of key, Maureen dismissed Cade's amorous adventures from her thoughts, and the old Dodge began to ascend the asphalt road lined with twisted oaks, squat cedars and expensive light poles. She passed a herd of longhorn cattle. Some ranch. Electric gates and lights, paved roads, designer cows. Conspicuous consumption. This rich man's retreat was a far cry from the accommodations she provided, both willingly and lovingly, for Cade's father.

She halted behind two automobiles of the six-figures variety, then got out to dust her blue suit and white pumps. Her faux leather handbag tucked at her side, she marched toward the two-story mansion of native stone. A few steps short of the double front door, she took a breath of clean country air for courage.

A sixtyish woman, with silver-shot flaxen hair and a crisp gray uniform, answered her summons. *"Ja?"*

"Maureen Miniver to see Mr. Herrington."

"You're the one who's been calling and calling Mr. Cade," the housekeeper commented in a German inflection.

"Yes, ma'am. But I assure you, he's expecting my visit."

"I know. And I'm glad for it." The rosiness in the older woman's cheeks deepened. "Ah, um, come this way, *Mädchen.*"

The housekeeper was glad for Maureen's visit? How strange. Or was it? Apparently the woman knew something about the situation and approved of a détente between Cade and Wilburn. At least that was Maureen's hope.

As she was ushered through the house, Maureen was pleasantly surprised by the surroundings. Upholstered leather furniture topped hooked rugs. Black and white photo enlargements of animals and people, as well as books and paintings, lined the walls. Vases of flowers abounded. An overweight marmalade cat sidled up to meow and purr, and to tangle around Maureen's ankle.

"Nice kitty," she cooed, scratching the feline's ear.

Everything about the house was inviting, like a long cool lemonade on a hot summer day. Funny. She had imagined her stepbrother living in a decorator's dream, such as the penthouse she remembered from that Christmas meeting.

"Elections are in August, Cade," rushed from beneath the den's closed door. "If you want—"

The housekeeper rapped her knuckles against the door, opened it to announce the visitor's presence, then closed it again to leave Maureen with the two men in the fireplace-dominated den.

The older man rose to his feet from a cushy, oversized chair. Last Friday, she had figured out his identity. He was Douglas Smythe, a lesser partner in Fortuna Enterprises and owner of half of South Texas.

A frown bracketing his mouth, his chin tucked down, Cade stood with the heel of his palm resting against the fireplace mantel. He pushed away and started toward her. His gold-flecked brown eyes, so unreadable in the past, were troubled. "Hello, Maureen."

"Cade," she murmured while covertly taking in his Western attire and rugged appearance. Levi's, boots and the yoked shirt looked marvelous on his lean frame, as if he were to the land born, which Maureen knew wasn't the case. His heritage was below the ground—oil not cattle.

"You've met Mr. Smythe." He motioned to the distinguished man who was past middle age. "But you weren't introduced."

As he continued, she noted that he didn't mention their family status. In a quandary, both by the friendly reception and the mystery of it, she marshaled the proper amount of cordiality, finishing with, "I didn't mean to interrupt another business conference."

"I assure you, we weren't talking Fortuna Enterprises." Cade held her elbow while leading the way to a huge cordovan sofa. "Doug and I are old friends."

What was going on here? Fireworks and problems—such had been her expectations. She wasn't prepared for hominess, or hooked rugs, or marmalade cats, and certainly not for cordiality.

What had happened to Mr. Mean of the previous Friday? She must be dreaming, or maybe she'd spent too much time in a hot van. "Cade..."

"We were just talking about you, Ms. Miniver."

What had they been saying about a baker from the wrong side of San Antonio's tracks? Settling into the sofa's rich embrace, she glanced from Cade to the other man. Mr. Smythe had the good manners not to peer at her, as Cade was doing. Racking her brain, she tried to recall all she had heard about the no-Texan-here Smythe. Wilburn, being the ear-to-the-ground type, had mentioned a couple of specifics on an occasion or two, but beyond Mr. Smythe's standing in the business community, she drew a blank. Some things were apparent, though. He reeked of money, the kind passed down from ancestors. His accent implied that he was from up North, definitely upper-class. What a strange combo they were, the man of refinement and the self-made millionaire born and reared in the dusty tumbleweeds of Midland, Texas.

But how had she come into the conversation?

"Don't keep me in suspense," she said. "I'm dying to know what my—" Out of Douglas Smythe's line of sight, her stepbrother was shaking his head to plead discretion. "What *Cade* had to say about me."

"Ah, my dear, nothing but the nicest things."

She wouldn't bet her lone pair of silk panties on that.

"Cade, Maureen, if you'll excuse me, I must be running along. Sandra expects me to squire her to the Ballet Folklorico tonight. Mustn't be late."

"Sandra is Doug's daughter," Cade explained.

Is that so? Maureen bade adieu to Smythe, all the while perplexed at the tension in Cade's face. Was Sandra the reason?

"May I fix you a drink?" he asked when they were alone. "Coffee, tea or something stronger?"

Why was he being the perfect host? Probably he was up to some trick, maybe along the lines of floating like a butterfly and stinging like a bee. Let him. After all, wasn't the queen bee the more powerful one? " 'Something stronger' will do."

Cade handed her a glass, their hands touching for a moment. His fingers were long, firm and rough-textured. She was surprised by the calluses—they didn't fit an oil magnate's image. But Cade was no Douglas Smythe. And despite her animosity toward him, she found the contrast of Cade—the hands of a workman and the success of a tycoon—intriguing.

He dropped into a chair opposite the sofa, lifted his feet to the coffee table and held his cup high. "Cheers."

Maureen sipped the mellow sour-mash whiskey. "I've done some thinking since last Friday." *Please let this work,* she prayed. "After I left your office, I had a long talk with myself, and put myself in your shoes, if you will. It's got to be tough, being plagued by someone you don't wish to be bothered by. You want Wilburn out of your hair, so wouldn't it be to your advantage to keep him from..." She sliced off "trying to" before saying, "...from calling and visiting?"

Cade eyed her over the rim of his cup. "Could be."

"If you help him get started in business, he'd go back to West Texas. You have plenty of money. What's fifty thousand dollars to you? A mere drop in the bucket." She took a breath before voicing a whopper lie. "You wouldn't see him again."

"You're trying to hustle me."

"Call it what you wish." She forced a smile. "Do you make contributions to charities?" she asked, knowing full well he did, according to Wilburn.

"I do. But I thought you were after a loan."

Darn, why did he bring that up? The last thing she needed was another obligation. "A loan wouldn't be in your best interest. Philanthropy would. Beyond the satisfaction of helping a needy cause, you'd be free of the problem. And you wouldn't have to worry whether I'd repay the loan."

Cade got to his feet and walked across the room to refill his cup. "I've decided—"

"Mr. Cade," the housekeeper put in after knocking before entering, "Mr. Doug is back." She led him into the den.

"Sorry to trouble you two. Have you seen my hat?"

The old snoop. He was not a convincing liar, and apparently Cade was of the same mind, measuring by the haste with which he escorted Douglas from the room.

Minutes ticked by. Maureen, anxious over Cade's decision, forced other thoughts. Cutter's Mill came to mind. How could she get herself in a financial position to offer the mystery owner a deal? First of all, she needed to get out of debt. No more diet colas and choice cuts of steak, both personal favorites; from now on it would be Kool-Aid and macaroni and cheese. No more fashion magazines that served no purpose, since she couldn't afford perfumes and fancy clothes, anyhow. Cable TV would have to go. But these were all stopgap measures. Of course, she *could* cut back on the expensive ingredients in her cookies.... No! That was out of the question.

She paced the rug, then went out to the adjacent wooden deck that ran along the back of the house and jutted over the hillside. There was a panoramic view of the rough, yet engaging countryside. Cumulus clouds darkened the sky. In spite of the warm breeze, she shivered.

What had Cade decided?

Apprehensive, she reentered his den and walked to the corner desk. She glanced at the desktop, and her heart took an extra beat while her shaking hand reached for a framed photograph. An unsmiling woman had her arm looped around the crook of a man's elbow as he held a young boy in the other. The reminder of old was a picture of Cade, his mother—and Wilburn. If Cade despised his father, he wouldn't have his picture on prominent display. He *did* care for him!

Ebullient, Maureen sat on the sofa again. Five minutes later her stepbrother returned, and she ventured, "You were going to tell me what you've decided...."

"I'll get to it in time."

She granted breathing space. "Mr. Smythe seems nice."

"He's the best. We've been friends for a long time, Maureen. If not for him, I wouldn't be where I am today."

It was strange, trying to picture Cade as a friend to anyone. For all these years she had pegged him as uncommunicative and brooding—what else did she have to go by but a couple of quick meetings and his attitude toward her beloved stepfather? "Is it friendship you feel, or a sense of obligation?"

"Call it a little of both."

Motivated by the look on Cade's face, she asked, "Is something wrong?"

He sat down and stared at her, his gaze holding hers for several moments. "I've got a problem."

"Wilburn?"

"No." He took a sip of cold coffee. "It's a woman."

Sandra, no doubt. "Someone you love?"

"In my own peculiar way."

"Come on, that's not a positive declaration of love."

Twice in one day Maureen had heard love mentioned with

less than full implications. Money really doesn't buy happiness, she concluded while itching to hear Cade's story. "You don't have the sound of a man struck silly by Cupid's arrow."

"I don't believe in love. But I do care about Sandra."

Bingo. Maureen took a moment to give herself a mental pat on the back for being astute. Then other thoughts came to mind. Lucky gal, that Sandra, receiving Cade's concern, which was something Wilburn was in dire need of. But the picture proved he had a heart. He wasn't all bad, was he?

"Love doesn't have to destroy," she murmured.

Outdoors, a soft rain began to fall; the room darkened, as if dusk were descending. Maureen waited for Cade to speak. He tapped his index finger on a touch-sensitive lamp base, bathing the room in warm, golden light, but he didn't reply.

Maureen studied his profile. His nose had a rather Roman outline, very attractive and manly. The contours of his tanned, square-jawed face were sculpted into masculine juts and angles that showed signs of a five o'clock shadow, and he was brushing his fingers across lips forming an uncurved line. He wasn't a pretty boy. His looks were rugged as the Texas terrain, yet his was a handsome face, resembling his father's, though Cade's visage was troubled.

Curious about this enigmatic man, she wondered why he wouldn't allow himself the glory of love. Right then Maureen felt a deep compassion for the man who had everything, yet nothing at all.

"Cade, simple caring can be a wonderful basis for building unselfish love."

"Aren't you wise?" There was a cutting edge to his tone; twin frown lines formed between his eyes. He stood and walked to the oversize sliding glass doors. "Blessed with all the answers...."

"No, I don't have all the answers. Why don't you do the talking? Tell me about your trouble with Sandra Smythe."

"Uhr. Sandra Uhr." He stared at his stepsister as though to ascertain her trustworthiness. Again taking his chair, he exhaled. "And I wouldn't call her trouble. She's more of a problem that I'd like to solve. I don't want to hurt her feelings. I want her to be happy."

"I'm not quite following you."

"Doug expects us to marry, which puts me in a ticklish situation. Since the Smythes are like family to me, I don't want to do anything to jeopardize our friendship. You see, I'm the son Doug never had, and he's disappointed I'm not jumping into baby's breath and 'Here Comes the Bride.'"

"You have to marry sometime. Why not Sandra?"

Cade centered his attention on Maureen. "I'm not the forever kind."

Why, why, why? "Does her dad know you don't love her?"

"Yeah. But to Doug's way of figuring, I'll idolize her once we're committed to each other."

"Doesn't she have some say in this?"

"She's of the same mind. Marriage. She's conveniently forgotten a small point. The husband she has already."

Maureen gasped. "How can she even consider...?"

"She's not your ordinary woman. Like the old song goes, 'What Lola wants, Lola gets.' The one time good old dependable Phil stood up to her, Sandra split the sheets. Now she's convinced it's all over between the two of them."

"If you ask me, she doesn't sound like a nice person."

"Wrong. Spoiled by easy money, I'll admit, but she's a great gal," he said sincerely. "Right now she's misguided in her emotions, but if she'd give Phil half a chance, they'd get back together. Especially if I'm out of the picture. So I'd like to do something to reconcile the Uhrs."

Responding to his compassion, Maureen cautioned, "By meddling in others' lives, you may be loosing a hive of trouble on yourself."

He looked away—to consider her advice? At last his dark eyes moved to her light ones. "You're right in principle, wrong in this case. I just want to give nature an opportunity to take its course." He paused. "That's where you come in. Doug's made a few incorrect assumptions about you. He figures we're involved romantically."

"Surely not— What gave him that idea?"

"Think about it. You tore into my office demanding your rights, then showed up here today. What else is he to think?"

"Cade Herrington, you'd better correct his assumptions, and you'd better do it fast."

"No."

Her warm feelings fizzled, but she made a high demand of herself. Patience. "Does he know we're related?"

"I told him when he came back for his 'hat.' But that doesn't stop Doug from imagining the worst. Needless to say, he's not pleased about our 'love,' but he'll recover."

"That ought to be easy enough," she answered dismissively. "We aren't in love."

"That's beside the point. He thinks I was brushing you off to protect Sandra. Why correct him? I see a means to an end."

Her curiosity was at full tilt. "What means to what sort of end?"

Cade claimed a spot on the sofa next to Maureen and slid a strand of hair behind her ear. The tingling sensation she felt was as unexplainable as his sudden coziness.

"How much are you willing to give of your time to help the needy cause of Wilburn Herrington?" he asked.

She drew away from herbal after-shave and warm male scents. "What are you asking me to do?"

"Participate in a hoax, and I'll make it worthwhile."

"Excuse me?"

"I want you to play the part of my beloved."

"Your beloved?" She shot to her feet. "Absolutely not. Never."

"Anyone ever tell you . . . you say and do things without thinking them through?"

All the time. "My behavior is *my* business."

"Business. Interesting subject." His head tilted to an angle of superiority. "You ought to save your absolutely-nots till after we discuss your bakery." He stood and confidently crossed to the desk, extracting a manila envelope from a drawer. "It didn't take long for my investigator to find out a lot about you and your cookie factory."

Shocked at his audacity, Maureen stared at the envelope. "How could you . . . ?"

"Very easily."

She stomped over to him and jabbed a forefinger against his pectoral. "You have an investigator on me? That's an underhanded trick."

"I'd say it's a smart move. I like to know who and what I'm dealing with." Thunder resounded through the room as he grabbed her fingers. "You run your business Wilburn-style, by the seat of your pants, and I'll use that information to its best advantage . . . if necessary."

"You're up to some sort of blackmail."

"Extortion never occurred to me."

Looking into his dark eyes, she asked, "What did occur to you?"

"That you're in no position to guarantee a loan for fifty bucks, much less one for fifty thousand."

She looked to the right. Pride wouldn't allow her to admit that his assessment was correct.

"I'm going to rephrase my offer, Maureen. If you want me to help ole Wil, I *expect* you to help me out."

Under normal circumstances she'd have gathered her purse and pride to make a run for it, but these were not normal circumstances, and she was there for a purpose.

"I might be willing to agree," she said. "As long as you'll do a lot of giving, where your father is concerned. Spend a weekend with him, and you'll have my free hours. For a couple of weeks."

"Is that so? Before, it was big dough. Today it's one weekend of my time." He paused. "You shouldn't sell yourself short. You should've held out for the money."

"Financial help goes without saying," she answered, determined to stand her ground. "I won't compromise."

His chuckle was low, harsh. "Okay, you win."

"Then we have a deal."

"Not so fast." His heated gaze melted into the blue of hers. "How far are you willing to go?"

Reading lascivious intent, she was halfway to the door before saying, "I'm not for sale, or hire!"

His roar of laughter whipped her around. "I wasn't asking for your favors, Maureen. I was testing your principles."

She jacked up her chin. "Be careful. You never know when you might get stung by a killer bee."

"Don't concern yourself with my well-being," he advised sternly. "I'll see after myself."

"Do that. And while you're at it, get someone else to participate in your scheme. I'm not interested."

"You're missing the point. Doug already thinks you and I are a hot item."

"Let him think what he pleases. Maybe you, Cade Herrington, should stop to do some thinking of your own. Have you given a thought to Sandra's feelings? She might not take kindly to being rejected."

"I know Sandra better than she knows herself."

"You've had a pretty hot romance going, eh?"

"Not at all. What I'm trying to tell you is, Sandra is a good but misguided woman, and she needs a boost in the right direction. What I'm proposing to you is for her benefit."

Maureen paused to study her stepbrother. "Are you being nice? Or are you a heel looking for an out?"

"A little of both."

"Personally, if I were Sandra, I'd say, 'Good riddance to bad rubbish.'"

"Who knows?" He laughed. "Maybe those will be her words."

He took Maureen's hand. "Why don't we back up a bit?" he asked, and his tone was considerably lighter. "My intentions weren't to hurt your feelings. All I want is a *damn convincing* business deal, one that's mutually advantageous. I'll give Wilburn all he wants, and you'll get something out of it, too. I'll invest in your cookie factory."

"Uh-uh. Let's get something straight. Granny Miniver's is a sole proprietorship, and it's going to stay that way."

"If that suits you." He didn't appear convinced. "Now, all you have to do is donate a couple of months of your time. In the role of my fiancée."

For once, Maureen was speechless.

Chapter Three

If she never laid eyes on Cade Herrington again, it would be too soon.

Since leaving his ranch last Sunday, Maureen had reflected on his odd proposal, and now, as she wound down the work week in her kitchen this Friday afternoon, she had her regrets. She should have told him no. A flat-out no, leaving no room for speculation on his part, instead of her mealy-mouthed, "I'll think about it."

Maureen twisted the top onto a quart-size bottle of vanilla flavoring, shoved it into a cabinet, then frowned. With her many bakery duties and her undeveloped plans to wrest Cutter's Mill from its owner, she didn't have time for Cade's malarkey. His clandestine investigation of her affairs was downright disgusting. Most importantly, being party to some elaborate hoax went against her principles.

Tonight she would tell him no. At eight this evening, when he was expected, she'd be free of her stepbrother.

She glanced at his father, who was helping her assistant with the heavy-duty flour mixer. Guilt became stronger than Maureen's aggravation and anxieties. If she told Cade where to stick his ridiculous ideas, where would she be in her plans to help dear Wilburn? Back at—

"Square one."

Janece Stewart's announcement, preceded by the air conditioner's sudden silence and a blackening of the oven-indicator light, pushed Maureen's dilemma aside. She turned to her employee and friend, a bespectacled redhead of thirty-five.

"The breaker again," Maureen grumbled.

"Yes."

"Step aside, my good woman," Wilburn said to the buxom and frowning Janece. "I'll take care of it."

She parked her fists on her hips. "That, my good man, is the problem. You wired up this damned oven, and you had no call splicing into the 220 wiring."

Inwardly Maureen had to agree, in light of the problems encountered all week with the electricity, but . . . "Jan!"

"It's true and you know it."

"Jan, he only had so much to work with. You know I can't afford a proper electrician."

"Some things have to be included in a budget." Janece whipped off her glasses. "That's the price of doing business."

"Pray tell, where did you get your economics degree?"

"Now, now, girls, settle down."

His suggestion gave Maureen pause. There was no excuse for her testiness. Huh! She did have a reason, and it was a four-letter word. C-A-D-E.

She took three steps toward the older woman. "I'm sorry."

"I apologize, too. I know how you..." Perching her half glasses back on her nose, Janece cast an arch look at the tall and lean, gray-haired object of her true pique. "Haven't you got better things to do, my dear Mr. Herrington, than to stand around gawking?"

"Yes, ma'am. Looks like I need to buy a new breaker box." He exited the back door.

Thankfully, the present batch of cookies had finished baking despite the power loss, and Maureen set them on the cooling rack, then poured glasses of lemonade for herself and Janece. Her hands shook.

"Something's wrong beyond a power blackout," Janece said speculatively. "Wanna tell me 'bout it?"

Maureen braced her palms on the countertop. To this point, she hadn't uttered a word to Wilburn about Cade, much less to anyone else. She needed to talk, wanted advice and needed relief badly. In words punctuated with deep sighs and head shakes, she told Janece about the confrontation with Cade. "I don't want to be mixed up in his scheme," she said at the end.

Janece lifted a shoulder. "What's the problem? Just tell him no, and be done with it."

"Easy for you to be flip. You don't have a stake in Wilburn's happiness."

"I wasn't being flip," Janece replied sincerely. "You know I have your best interest at heart. I can tell you have your doubts, and I think you should put yourself ahead of anyone else. Which isn't like you at all, but . . ."

"It'll make me happy if Wilburn's happy."

Janece frowned, and Maureen wasn't surprised—more than once, Janece had voiced disapproval of Wilburn. She knew the older woman believed she was being taken advantage of by his living with her, but Maureen wasn't seeking approval. "I love Wilburn, and that's the most important thing."

"Then I revise my advice. Tell Cade yes, and make the most of it."

"Yuck."

Plopping down in a chrome-and-plastic kitchen chair, Janece folded her arms and settled her elbows on the Formica-topped table. "All right, let's take this from the top. You don't like the deceit of his phony engagement plans. You've never told a lie?" Not waiting for an answer, she went on. "Seems to me you're doing a fair share of it, promising Cade that all you want is financial help for Wilburn."

Maureen considered those words. "You're right, I suppose. But I'm mad at Cade for siccing his gumshoe on Granny Miniver's."

"You're just sensitive about this cookie factory. Nothing wrong with that, mind you, but don't you figure Cade got where he is by being shrewd? Can you fault a man for finding an advantage and using it?"

"When it involves me, yes."

Janece shook her head in exasperation. "Okay, let's look at this from another angle. Cade's willing to go along with you on this Wilburn thing, so you'll be getting what you want. He wants to help what's-her-name, and he feels like he's got to make it convincing. Seems reasonable. She'll think she still has a chance if he merely takes up with another woman. An 'engagement' does have a ring of sincerity, you have to admit."

Perspiration trickled down Maureen's face, and she picked up a paper plate to fan herself. "Honestly, Sandra isn't my problem. Why should I care what happens to her? I don't even know the woman."

"Since Cade's willing to put out money and effort for Sandra and hubby to kiss and make up, he really must care for that gal, since you and I both know he doesn't give a snap for Wilburn." She paused. "I think Cade is to be admired."

"His motives are admirable where she's concerned," Maureen conceded, realizing she was weakening. "It seems he has a rather brotherly attitude toward her."

"Do I detect a bit of sibling jealousy, pray tell?"

"Not in the least. He's not really my brother. And if he's honorable enough to help Sandra, he's capable of mending fences with Wilburn."

"If that's how you feel, you are one silly girl not to do what you can to bring that about."

"Call me crazy, call me a fool, but, Jan, I can't just up and devote hour upon hour to Cade. You know how busy I am with this bakery, and I've got to find time for my Cutter's Mill plans."

"Cutter's Mill? Bah! That's so far in the future it can't be a problem for now. As for this cookie factory, I've had three years to study you, my friend. Three years of your dedication to making a go of it. It's time you broadened your horizons. Think about what Cade's offering. It's not a bad deal. And who knows? You might enjoy a few dates at a lot of ritzy places." Janece added, "Don't let pride stand in the way of your objective. Give Cade Herrington a chance."

Wilburn stepped into the kitchen. "What's this about my boy?"

"Please work on the electricity," Maureen requested to delay the inevitable. Honesty was necessary—but not in front of Janece. "It's an oven in here, no pun intended."

He opened his mouth, then closed it before doing as asked.

"Jan, on your way home, will you deliver these cookies to Simon's Bakery?"

"You betcha." She collected the trolley, stacked boxed cookies on it, and gave Maureen a hug of support. "Good luck, kiddo, whatever you decide to do."

Janece departed. The air conditioner kicked on and the oven's red indicator light brightened. Maureen set about preparing the week's final batch of cookies. Wilburn returned to the kitchen, question and concern looming in his craggy features.

"Sugar Pie, what's going on with my son?"

"You'd better sit down."

During the next twenty minutes, as Maureen gave him the facts and continued to busy herself, Wilburn was unusually noncommittal. After putting the last of the cookies into the oven, she turned to him. "What do you think?"

He ran his fingers through his thick gray hair that had the same texture as his son's black hair. "Can't say I approve of you going to Cade like that, but I appreciate what you were trying to do," he admitted, his voice gravelly. "But, when Cade and I are together, Maureen, I'd like to know he's with me because—well, I want it to be from his heart."

"That's my objective, too."

Squinting, Wilburn turned his gaze away from his stepdaughter. "Don't get involved."

"I'm already involved."

"Get uninvolved, Sugar Pie. Me and my boy, we'll get back together someday. And on our own."

She felt as if a weight had been lifted from her shoulders. Wilburn would handle his son. With a clear conscience, she'd tell Cade no. Everything was simple.

Suddenly, the cooling unit ceased operation again, as did the oven indicator light. Smoke rushed from the oven door's perimeters and the smell of melting electrical elements permeated the room, rousing chokes from Maureen and her stepfather. Wilburn jerked the oven door open, and flames shot toward the ceiling. Maureen bolted for the fire extinguisher.

Two hours later, after the firemen had left, chaos settled down to relative calm. The fire had been contained to the kitchen, but smoke and the water from fire hoses had damaged the other rooms and their contents. Everywhere the stench of destruction lingered.

Maureen, with smudges on her face and arms, collapsed into a folding chair on the front porch and eyed her stepfather, who had his head tucked down.

"That fire was all my fault," Wilburn agonized.

"Don't blame yourself," she pleaded, not for the first time since the fire brigade had departed. Rubbing at her smudges with a wet rag and wrinkling her nose against the smells emitting from the house, she said, "If anyone is to blame, it's me. I should've hired an electrician."

"Don't make excuses for me." His tired eyes settled on hers. "I don't deserve your patience and understanding."

"Why not? You've always been that way with me. Like the time I knocked the TV over just before the seventh game of the World Series. Like the time I crashed your go-cart. Like the time I snuck out to meet that horrid biker." She waited for his usual chuckle. Fruitlessly.

"You were a kid then, and those things don't compare to what I've done to you. Granny Miniver's is kaput."

"Nope. It's down but not out. No fire can take away what I have up here." She tapped her head. "I'll be back in business in no time."

How that would be accomplished was a scattered, thousand-piece puzzle. Not to mention accounts payable and slow receivables, what would they do for income until she got set up again? How would she meet Janece's salary? She had insurance, of course, but the deductible was high.

A more immediate problem reared its head. Her purse held fifty dollars, her bank account little more, and her VISA card was embracing its limit. How would they clothe themselves? Get by? Where would they live?

She heard a car motor and spied a white Bentley roll to a stop in front of her burned-out house. Drat. In the hub-bub, she had forgotten Cade was expected at eight. Weren't matters bad enough already?

Wearing Italian loafers and casually elegant attire, he folded long arms across his chest and stared. Several seconds passed before he started the fifteen-foot journey to Maureen's front porch.

He scanned the smoky windows. "Is this a new problem?" he asked her.

"Exceedingly."

"Hello, son."

"Wilburn," Cade returned curtly. Half turning to Maureen, he furrowed his black brows. "You're not hurt, are you?"

"No. And Wilburn isn't, either."

"What happened?" he asked as Wilburn walked to the end of the porch. Upon receiving his answer, which was punctuated by his father's unasked-for admission of culpability, Cade frowned. "You're in a helluva mess."

"Brilliant deduction," she said under her breath.

Wilburn spoke. "Yes, son, we're in a pickle right now, but everything's gonna be all right."

"Talk is cheap."

"Son, don't speak to me like—" The elder Herrington clamped his mouth.

Cade stood with his fists clenched. Tension galvanized from him with the intensity of an electrical current, and

Maureen covered her lips with twitching fingers. Last Friday, Cade had said he disliked his father because he was a dreamer. If only Wilburn would prove that he was more than talk.... But he couldn't prove a thing without opportunity. And Cade might never grant another opportunity.

She just couldn't stand back and do nothing. It was going to take patience and mediation for a healing of old wounds. An outsider's patience and mediation. Trouble was, Maureen was too distraught to play peacemaker.

"You'd best leave, Cade." She pushed a strand of sooty dark-brown hair from her temple. "Your father and I have things to do."

Cade walked over to peer into the window. "You won't be doing anything in there. It's obvious you can't stay here. Where will you go?"

Maureen licked her lips.

"We'll find a place," Wilburn said.

"A motel?" Cade asked.

Maureen looked away.

"Janece Stewart will take us in," Wilburn assured her.

"Y-yes, that'll work." Maureen's words were as empty as her pockets, since Janece lived with her elderly mother in a one-bedroom flat.

"I've got plenty of room," Cade said, astounding Maureen. "You can stay with me."

"Now, son, that won't be necessary."

"Seems to me it's very necessary," was Cade's comment.

Why in heaven's name was he making his offer? But now wasn't the time to voice her question. Not in front of Wilburn.

"Yes, or no, Maureen?" Cade implored.

It was on the tip of her tongue to add her own protest, but she bit off her words. After all, Cade had offered Wilburn quarters in his home. Time together might be the answer, might give Wilburn and his wayward son a chance to heal their raw, raw wounds. No, darn it, she decided "might" wasn't a strong enough word. Time together *would* cure all ills.

And since she had decided, at Wilburn's urging, not to accept Cade's ludicrous deal, she needed an alternate plan—one that didn't include a sham engagement.

She swallowed her pride and forced a smile. "Thank you, Cade. We accept."

"Maureen Miniver, we'll do no such thing!"

A muscle tightened in Cade's face. "For once, think of someone beyond yourself. Thanks to you, Maureen's lost her home and business."

Wilburn bowed his head.

And thank you for making Wilburn feel even worse. She reached for Wilburn's cold hand. "It's only till we find another place."

He nodded.

"Follow me." Cade started down the steps, but stopped and turned to her. "But you know the way, don't you?"

Yes, she knew the way to the Dry Hole Ranch, but momentarily she questioned the probable success of her mission. Was the rift too deep between father and son for a reunion? That train of thought was unacceptable to Maureen Miniver. It was unreasonable to expect too much in a few short minutes, and certainly not under these circumstances.

She'd make the best of a bad situation.

After she followed Cade to his ranch, with a reluctant Wilburn trailing along in his beat-up tan Pontiac, she settled in to a suite of rooms in the ranch house's east wing, then showered and dressed. Thankfully, three laundry baskets of clothes had been discovered in the trunk of the Blond Bomber, her pet name for Wilburn's car. Weren't they lucky, she reflected, that Wilburn neglected to put away their laundry?

She slipped into the brown espadrilles that were her only pair of footwear, thanks to the fire, then drew on a blue terry-cloth romper. She pulled a face at her white legs. Oh, for the luxury of a nice tan.... Well, she was a working woman, not some member of the rich-and-bored set with lazy hours to brown in the sun, file her fingernails and bark at the hired help. None of which appealed to her, anyhow. She had no reason to be ashamed of her pale legs or short-clipped nails.

Her hair damp, she entered Cade's study...at his behest, as relayed by a servant.

There was a taut look on his angular face, and he was holding the fat, orange and brown cat who had sidled up to Maureen on her first visit to the Dry Hole. The feline leaned its chin into his caressing fingers. Maureen was astounded. Even though she knew he owned this animal, never had she imagined Cade as a cat person.

There were a lot of things about him beyond her imagining, she supposed.

"Do I have an answer?" he asked Maureen, while giving her legs a quick once-over. He hiked up a black brow and glanced away.

No doubt he compared her legs unfavorably to those of the women in his set. Why did that bother her?

"By your silence," he said, "I take it you haven't made up your mind. I'll give you till Sunday. Not a day longer." Cade set the huge cat on its paws, then began to pace the hooked rug. "Doug Smythe is planning a barbecue at his lake cottage, and I've already told him we'll be there. We're expected at one sharp. Sunday."

Already told him? Expected? Although Maureen was grateful for Cade's concession on living arrangements, she ground her teeth at his presumptuousness.

"In the meantime, make yourself at home," he said. "I'll be at my penthouse."

"You aren't staying here?"

"I'm not."

Her plans for a father-son parley were falling apart! "But, but—since you were planning to take off, why did you invite us to be your guests?"

"You're forgetting I had you and your bakery investigated. I know you're broke, and that Stewart woman needs houseguests like the Pope needs religious instruction." Cade leaned a narrow hip against the oaken desk, crossed his ankles and rested his knuckles against his waist. "Furthermore, if old Wil ever had a dime, he'd toss it in the air and run under it."

The Pollyanna outlook she had promised to espouse took a nosedive. "We've been poor a long time. You never showed any charity before."

"Never had a reason to, before. Come on, Maureen, think about it. I have a vested interest in your welfare. Couldn't have my fiancée sleeping on a curb, could I?"

"I'm not your—" Seething, but not surprised by the man who had castigated his father to his face, she took a step closer to the contrary tycoon. "So... my sleeping alfresco wouldn't look good on your personal profit-and-loss statement, right?"

"You might say that."

Patience. Remember your objective. She smiled sweetly, the effort fairly cracking her cheeks. "It was awfully nice of you to take us in. We appreciate your generosity. Wilburn's in the kitchen right now. Why don't I call him? He'll want to have a word with you before you leave."

Cade's brow furrowed. "Don't be too sure of yourself, Maureen—at least where Wilburn Herrington is concerned. You presume to second-guess his frame of mind, and that's dangerous territory."

"I've nothing to fear. I know Wilburn."

"Then you have my sympathies." Cade picked up a brass paperweight and studied it. "But let's not get off track. I know what you're trying to do. You're trying to hog-tie me to him, but it won't work." He paused. "Not until I have your word to our bargain."

"I won't be—" She swallowed. Eyes downcast, she shuffled her feet. For some weird reason, she wanted to express her misgivings and grievances before telling him no—maybe for his understanding? "Cade, with Granny Miniver's burned out, I don't have time for social engagements."

"Seems to me you have all the time in the world. You'll be doing a bunch of things differently, now and in the future, so why not include our joint venture in your schedule?"

"Because I resent your snooping into my business."

"So, that's the crux of it." He rubbed his chin. "Maureen, since the minute you barged into my office, you've been full of demands. I don't know you, not really. And I certainly don't care for your style, as it relates to that old man."

She took a step toward Cade. "Since you feel that way, why do you want me in on your engagement scam?"

Dead quiet reigned for countless seconds before he replied, "You were convenient, and you've got a stake in the deal."

She wouldn't argue the last, but being called convenient stung. Why should it matter, what he thought of her? She tried to make sense out of it and decided she was too shaken over the fire to be sane.

"Surely you can see my side, Maureen. If you'd been in my position, what would you've done?"

"I wouldn't have hired some Dick Tracy to meddle in your affairs."

Shaking his head, Cade said, "Let me give you a secret to success. Know your competition and keep abreast of his strengths and weaknesses. Do you get my drift?"

"I do." Maureen hugged her arms, remembering Janece's comment about Cade getting to where he is by being shrewd. Plus, viewing her hot-pepper demands from his point of view, she did understand his calculated reasoning. "You wanted the upper hand and knew how to get it."

"Smart gal."

"Smart, maybe. Aggravated, absolutely."

He levered away from the desk to stand in front of her. His fingers moved to the lobe of her ear, then slid to her nape. "Does using my resources qualify me for jerk-of-the-year?" he asked, as a wicked smile eased across his handsome face and an involuntary shiver wound from her head to her toes.

"No. Anyhow, it's in the past and best forgotten. Especially under the circumstances." Feeling strangely rotten, she stared at the toes of her sandals. "To be honest, Cade," she admitted quietly, "I've decided not to accept your offer."

Several seconds passed. "Any reason in particular?" he asked, somewhat offhandedly. "Beyond those you mentioned."

"Because your father disapproves."

"Fine. You've just saved me a wad of money."

It was settled, yet . . . she couldn't quite bring herself to turn away from Cade. And where did all this leave Wilburn and the reconciliation he needed with his son? Nowhere. And that wouldn't do.

Even though her stepfather had discouraged her involvement, she wouldn't throw in the towel. She just couldn't! But was it too late to make something out of nothing?

Her throat constricted, yet she managed to ask, "What will you do about Sandra?"

Cade's eyes settled on Maureen's. "Do you care?"

His uncharacteristically soft tone caused Maureen to assess him from the tip of his loafers to the top of his tall and lean frame. She was well acquainted with this stance; it was the same as his father's, when Wilburn didn't want others to know the depth of his troubles. With another facet of Cade's personality revealed, Maureen reasoned that he wasn't nonchalant—losing this battle bothered him.

"I'm not a heartless person," she replied at last, her voice vibrating.

He exhaled his held breath. "Maureen, would you like to reconsider my offer?"

Relieved at the second chance, she closed her eyes momentarily. She would agree to Cade's hoax engagement. Wilburn might not approve, but he was the one to gain from all this; he'd simply have to understand her intentions.

Her acceptance didn't roll from her throat, though, thanks to the gravity of what she'd be doing, and for courage she walked to a corner of the study. Her eyes stopped on a framed photograph, and her pulse began to race as she took the frame into her hand. She recognized the young blonde.

Answering Cade slipped from her mind. "Who...who is this?"

"Sandra."

"Sandra?" she repeated incredulously. "It...it can't be. Surely it can't."

"Surely it is."

Good heavens. If the woman in the picture was Sandra Uhr, then... Maureen's sympathetic feelings toward the poor little rich girl resurfaced.

"Cade, I know Sandra. I—I met her one day at Cutter's Mill." The gristmill! "*You* own Cutter's Mill," Maureen exclaimed, her concentration diverted.

"Right."

"What... what are your plans for it?"

"Profit."

"Then you might be willing to sell?" she asked, hopeful as a beggar to a nobleman. Or to a tycoon, in this case.

"What the devil has that got to do with the subject matter? Or is this your way of saying no?"

For three years she had nurtured her dreams for the gristmill. Three long years. And now, with this turn of events, Maureen was loath to push aside those dreams for even a fraction of a minute. Hadn't Janece, who had a good head on her shoulders, advised to put herself ahead of everyone else? Well, she would. Just this once.

"I have a reason for asking about Cutter's Mill," she answered. "I'd like to know if it's for sale. I want to buy it." *Someday.*

Cade frowned. "Maureen, everything I've got is on the market, provided I get the right price."

"What's your price?"

"Out of your league. All the cookies in South Texas wouldn't finance that piece of property."

"It isn't that valuable," she protested.

"It is to me. Surveys look good for a pool of oil."

Being a native West Texan and a child of the oil fields, she didn't take umbrage at his priorities—fossil fuel over a deserted old building. Texas was the land of steel rigs, and the natives' golden understanding of the state's most lucrative asset. She understood his reasoning. She did, nonetheless, resent his assumption that Granny Miniver's would never be profitable enough to purchase her dream.

How could she get her hands on money, lots of money? There had to be a way, because her cookie factory *would* rise from the ashes, literally, to begin operations anew at Cutter's Mill. Nothing else was acceptable. But how would she do it? Suddenly she recalled Wilburn's words of the morning he'd bought that dratted oven. Why not sell the licensing rights to Granny Miniver's Famous?

She hated the concept, relinquishing the Granny Miniver name and her pride in its debatable success, but sometimes one had to sacrifice pride to achieve an objective. A sale to Texas Bakeries would provide funds for a new bakery, and it might be enough for a down payment.... She needed to buy time. On credit.

She imparted her most winning smile; unfortunately it was wasted on Cade's centurion profile. "I don't need the entire two hundred acres. I'd like to put an option on the gristmill and a couple of surrounding acres."

"No way. The best seismos were recorded in that area."

Talking an oilman out of a sure bet was as likely as a mother turning against her child, but Maureen had to try. "To sink a discovery well, the building would have to be razed."

"That's not a big deal."

"No, I suppose not," she retorted with forced airiness. "I don't imagine budgeting is ever a consideration when Fortuna Enterprises jumps into a project."

"Wrong."

"Then I stand corrected." She wet her lips. "Cade, I'm no expert in geology, but won't you be facing a large amount of money for exploration? Wildcatters have never been keen on Comal County."

"Maureen, I know my business."

"You didn't get rich by not knowing it. Gosh, you're the modern-day whiz of Texas oil. Risk is the name of your game, after all. Back in the twenties, didn't everyone scoff when Sid Richardson decided to drill in West Texas? We all know how that turned out—fantastically. Just like your many successes." *That's right. Lay it on thick. Wouldn't Mama be proud?* "I admire your accomplishments," she added earnestly.

"Cut the flattery, Maureen. Get to the point."

"Seismographics are no guarantee of oil, so why gamble?" She straightened her back. "Sink the discovery well on the second-best tract, and give me an option on the mill."

"And what do I get in return?"

"A 'fiancée.'"

He closed the distance between them, stopping two paces in front of her, and there was a look akin to loathing in his penetrating gaze. "Well, sweetheart," he said, his tone holding no inflection of endearment, "looks like I've just found your selling price."

"It . . . I didn't mean it to sound as if—"

"You'd better be worth it."

Maureen backed away from Cade's ominous words and glare, but there was no backing out of a deal done. For all her bravado to this moment, for all her silly thoughts about floating like a butterfly and stinging like a bee, she realized her shaky position. In this battle of wits, will and Wilburn, was she in over her head?

Chapter Four

Maureen had little time to contemplate her anxieties about Cade's mood swing from friendly persuasion to ill-concealed contempt—not with his curt demand that they had ground rules to discuss. The sooner, the better.

Cade, scowling, led her out of the study. "I had a cold dinner fixed for you. We'll make it a twosome now, since I want to get these things sorted out."

Maureen's stomach was knotted, and she wasn't hungry in the least, but she didn't protest as Cade escorted her to the informal dining room. What with his concession on Cutter's Mill, she should have been elated. She wasn't. Not with her demand weighing on her mind and heart. A "fiancée" for a gristmill had sounded self-serving. Sounded? Huh.

Further, she shouldn't be bothered recalling Cade's growled "You'd better be worth it." But she was troubled by it.

"Did I ask too much?" she asked, her quiet voice driven by a conscience that screamed, *Yes, you did*.

He laughed, half turning to peer at her, but his chuckle didn't meet his eyes. A prism of light from the chandelier cast his features in granite-hard relief. Taking pains not to touch her, Cade seated Maureen in a ladder-back chair, then faced the buffet and opened a bottle of white wine. "No," he answered at last, "you didn't ask too much. You did the smart thing, holding out for what *you* wanted."

"Cade, I know I sounded greedy, I know I did, but...just last week, you accused me of speaking before thinking, and I'm guilty of that."

He seated himself opposite Maureen. For long, ominous moments, silence stretched. She waited, unable to breathe, for Cade to reply. But he didn't.

His muscles strained the oxford-cloth shirt as he leaned forward to pour wine. Liquid tinkled into the glasses—the only sound in the room. He lifted a lid from a plate of cold cuts and distributed slices of wafer-thin turkey and ham to their plates. The palpable tension between him and Maureen escalated.

She couldn't stand it. "Cade...please say something."

"You almost had me fooled." His tone was even and measured, yet disappointment painted his expression. "I was beginning to think you were all you pretended to be— the kind of woman worth a real engagement...to some lucky man. The kind of gal any fellow would want in his camp, all fire and spirit and selfless determination. Oh, you've got the fire and spirit and determination, but in the final analysis you're like all the rest. Out for number one."

Offended by his superior, judgmental attitude, Maureen's guilt vanished. "Isn't that the pot calling the kettle black?" she asked, but couldn't get his words out of her mind. Assessing the whole statement, she backed off. "Your bitterness has to come from... I don't know, maybe a big disappointment in the past? Like major woman trouble."

"A man doesn't gain on his thirty-fifth birthday without getting burned, Maureen. Happens all the time. I'm no exception. But I consider my experiences lessons in life."

She studied her plate, and never for a moment did she believe those last blasé remarks.

"Look, let's forget it, shall we?" He reached for his fork. "A deal cut is a deal done, and we're business partners. We don't have to like each other, but we do have to act like it...if we're going to be successful with Sandra. She's all that matters to me."

He took a sip of wine. "We have to convince her that you and I were destined for each other. That a wedding is in the offing. That we're planning to spend the rest of our lives together. That we're...that we're in love." He paused. "Maureen, we can't act as if we're adversaries. For Sandra and Doug and everyone else connected to them, you and I must be convincing that we're on the level. Get my drift?"

"Lovebirds, in other words." After his nod, she frowned. "Will you be able to act the part, feeling the way you do about me?"

"How do you presume I feel about you?"

She fidgeted. "You never liked me to begin with, and now...after Cutter's Mill...I—I..."

"I never said I don't like you. To tell the truth, I've always found you rather charming."

She was taken aback by his praise, but... "You're angry with me for attaching strings to the 'engagement.'"

"I was. But I'm getting over it. I don't know, Maureen, I guess I was taking it personally when I should've been thinking along business lines. And this is a purely business arrangement."

"Yes, it is."

"All right, we've gotten that out of the way. Let's discuss you." His finely sculpted mouth eased into a quarter smile. "Will that be so difficult, acting as if I'm not an ogre?"

She scanned his tanned features, the thick black hair, the dark eyes that had faint lines radiating from the corners and were welded to hers. Cade was easy to look at. Compassion for Sandra was a plus on his side. There was the gristmill, not to mention his promises regarding his father. And that hint of vincibility she had discovered when he mentioned his past. Most importantly, Maureen wasn't without feminine emotions.

"No, it won't be difficult."

"Good. That'll make it easier for both of us." He took a bite of sliced turkey, then said, "Now, I'll tell you what I intend to do and what I expect of you."

Expect. His favorite word again. Cade had every right to expect a lot from her, and if their joint venture was to be a success, she had to quit being antagonistic. "I'm all ears."

"Good. Listen closely. I don't want to repeat myself. I intend to put you back in business. No strings attached."

"No."

"Yes."

"No. You've given me what I want."

"You're a woman of simple needs," he commented and pulled in the grin that formed. Solemn again, he straightened his shoulders. "Ever heard the expression 'He who has the gold makes the rules'? If you want to play the game, we do it my way. I want your undivided attention, except when you're doing your thing with Granny Miniver's, and you can't do that if you're fighting to make ends meet."

"I don't take charity."

"Consider it a loan."

"I'm finding this impossible to believe."

Shaking her head, she wondered if she was caught in some sort of Cinderella fantasy. She didn't want to be some poor, pitiable wretch needing rescue by a handsome and wealthy prince. Independence and the chance to prove herself on her own were what she wanted.

Beyond her own wants, she tried to reason out Cade's. "Why in the name of heck are you willing to lay out so much just for a friend to kiss and make up with her husband?"

He sipped his wine; his eyes bored into Maureen. At last he spoke. "So much? All I'm expending is money and a bit of time. Money—that's not an object. As for time, I'm willing to give it—for a cause I deem important. When I go after something, Maureen, I get it. And I'm tired of arguing with you over my motives. I've agreed to your terms, and I expect you to agree to mine. 'Nuff said."

How could she argue against the money and power behind a mule-headed man set on a cause? Here she was, a homeless and pitiable *wretch,* trying to keep her pride when others counted on her. Wilburn. Janece. Granny Miniver's customers. Admit it, she told herself, Cade's help would be a salvation. It was, nonetheless, bitter medicine.

Swallowing her pride, she said, "All right. A loan it is. It was nice of you to offer. Thank you."

He ignored her thanks and got to the point. "Were you able to save your business records?"

"I grabbed them before your dad and I ran from the fire."

"Good. I want my accountants to have a look at your books."

"I . . . I'm sure my records are fine."

"If they were *fine,* you wouldn't be in a financial mess, Maureen. I'll put someone on them tomorrow." He pushed his plate aside. "You'll need a place to live. Here at the ranch will do, and it won't cost you a dime. Make use of the pool in your free time. If you ride, you'll find a stable of horses to choose from."

"I'm not a woman of leisure." *But a tan and a ride on a horse does sound nice.* She was only human.

"Take time for relaxation. Too much work and worry will make you old before your time. But I do realize you have your cookie enterprise to consider. My kitchen is large enough for your operation and it's already equipped with two industrial ovens. You won't be getting in my house-keeper's way. Frieda doesn't cook much. So...*mi casa es su casa.*"

"That's generous of you," she managed to reply.

"Tell me," he prompted, "what do you feel is your greatest strength where business is concerned? And your greatest weakness."

She contemplated his question. "I'm more comfortable with the baking. I've always enjoyed it. The bookkeeping is rather enjoyable—I like to know where I stand at all times. As for my weakness... When I began Granny Miniver's, I had to teach myself to be the salesman, and I've never liked that aspect of the business."

"Hire a salesman. I'll pay him or her."

"Cade...you're awfully nice to offer the moon," she said truthfully, "but I don't need a salesman."

"No arguments, understand? Another thing. As my 'fi-ancée,' you'll need to dress the part. That means a new wardrobe."

All of this was too much for Maureen, yet she marshaled her dignity. "My...my clothes are all right."

"Don't take offense. Your clothes are fine, but most of your belongings just went up in flames. Meet me tomor-row, say around ten, at North Star Mall, and we'll make a run through Saks. And I don't want any arguments out of you!"

She had to bite her tongue not to protest. But she realized several things. She had a lot to be thankful for, and without Cade, she would be in deep trouble. Others, too, would gain from this crazy engagement—Wilburn, Sandra, Sandra's husband. And it was time Maureen started appreciating her benefactor.

Except in his past relationship with his father—which would change as soon as he made good on his promise to spend time with the elder Herrington—Cade was a doggone good guy.

At that moment his orange-and-brown cat put its front paws on Cade's thigh and reared up to beg a scrap of his food.

"Get down, Fifi, old girl," he said warmly. "You're showing bad manners."

Disobedient, Fifi batted his arm and emitted a caterwaul.

Maureen laughed. She liked Cade the cat lover. "All right, 'fess up. You hand-feed that cat."

"It's not good for her." An abashed expression on his face, he lifted a shoulder. "We're old friends. I can't help spoiling her."

"Doesn't make you all bad." Maureen rose and went around to the other side of the table. Kneeling down, she swiped a morsel of turkey from his plate and offered it to the obese cat. "I like animals, myself."

"Don't set your sights on the Feef," he warned lightly. "She's a one-person cat."

Fifi proved totally unreliable. She purred and arched her whiskered jaw against Maureen's wrist prior to curling against her leg.

"One-person cat, hmm?" Maureen teased.

"Well, she was."

Maureen's fingers caressed the abundant fur, and she thought, *How easily the two of us sell out. You for a bite of meat, me for a chance at Cutter's Mill.* She told herself not to think along those lines. Yes, she would accept Cade's good grace over the mill and his financial assistance. But every dime he advanced would be repaid. Every dime.

Right then the cat moved away from Maureen and jumped onto Cade's lap. He laughed in triumph, stroking her ear as he said, "I knew you wouldn't let me down."

"Cade Herrington, you're a softy for animals."

"Animals can be counted on."

"As opposed to people who do let you down?"

His fingers stilled. "Right."

Maureen was no psychologist, but she knew enough to grasp a concept. People who trusted animals over people had been hurt badly. Who had hurt Cade? Obviously he and his father had problems, but Wilburn had made every effort to show Cade his love. Surely his mother hadn't disappointed him. From all accounts, Rowena had been a mother bear about her cub. Did his distrust stem from a romance gone sour?

Normally Maureen would have pressed the subject, but since she was making strides with Cade, she wouldn't antagonize him with delving questions. Knowing more about him was what she wanted, but time was on her side. One thing she knew for certain. For six years she had resented his attitude toward Wilburn and had pegged Cade for nothing more than a coldhearted, calculating man. But there was more to him than that. Beneath his reserve lay a tender, fracturable heart. A heart that went out to poor Sandra and would give dear Wilburn a chance.

Looking into his gold-flecked brown eyes, she murmured, "Thank you, Cade. Thank you for everything."

She pushed to stand, and in doing so, brushed against his warm, solid thigh. She was shaking. His hand reached to steady her—and a jolt of emotion shot through every cell in her body. What was happening to her?

"Don't thank me. Just don't disappoint me," he whispered. "Good night, Maureen."

"Good night, nurse!" Janece parked her hands on her hips and shook her head. "I've never seen so many clothes in one place, outside of a dress shop, that is."

"Please, don't make me feel worse about them." Maureen dropped onto the bed in her temporary bedroom. "I tried to talk Cade out of buying all this stuff."

Janece picked up an ivory-hued linen suit. "All I've got to say is, when you agree to a deal, you strike a deal! Mmm, mmm, did you make a good one."

Saturday afternoon was waning. Maureen's feet throbbed; her nerves were on edge. She wished Janece would go home, or *somewhere* beyond the gates of Cade's ranch. "Don't you need to make up an order for the restaurant supply store?"

"I get the picture," Janece replied. "You want to be left alone with your horde."

"Actually, I need to figure up my debt."

A half minute later, Maureen was alone. She stared at the multitude of boxes and sacks that littered the large room. A ray of sunlight bounced off one box's gold lettering. HOUSE OF PIERRE it read. Saks Fifth Avenue hadn't been the only store where she and Cade had shopped. He bought garments in each of the expensive establishments North Star Mall had to offer. When her feet had turned to the modestly priced boutiques, Cade had steered her away. Upon finishing, the total bill for dresses, suits, shoes, handbags, swimsuits, cosmetics, accessories—she'd refused to shop for lingerie with him, flat-out *refused!*—had reached the gross national product. She'd have to sell a jillion cookies to repay Cade.

Her mushroom cloud of debt wasn't the sole cause of her distress. After Cade departed the previous evening, she remembered promising Wilburn not to meddle in his relationship with Cade. She had gone to her stepfather's room, but he was sleeping, so she'd put off telling him about the so-called engagement. This morning he took off before she awoke, delaying her speech. With each passing moment, her anxiety grew.

Of course, she should have been happy. Her goal to get father and son back together was progressing, and Granny Miniver's Famous would be operational again by Monday...thanks to Cade.

After they had drained the mall of its finest ensembles, Cade had driven her to his office. A cadre of hirelings awaited. Her insurance adjuster, as well as her landlord, had made an appearance. Like a genie, Cade had snapped his fingers and his every wish was a command.

The representative of Al Assurers and the landlord—who had been threatening a lawsuit over the fire—were dealt with first. At a round-table discussion, accountants had combed the soot-edged ledgers, giving their opinions and offering advice, which Maureen agreed with. Then the attorney charged with drawing up the Cutter's Mill option agreement had sat down at the conference table.

Lastly, Ted Taylor, experienced baked-goods salesman, was summoned from an outer office. Cade uttered nary a word as she pulsed Ted about his qualifications. She offered the eager young man a job.

Cade Herrington could move mountains on a Saturday afternoon, she reflected, and paced the bedroom floor. He was amazing. And intriguing. Utterly intriguing. *Surely you're not falling for the man who's given his father so much grief!* But Cade wasn't the heel she had always imagined. Heavenly days, what was happening to her? "I need fresh air."

Maureen sat by the creek that ran through Cade's ranch, the sun a tangerine slash above a hill to her right. Under an oak's canopy of leaves, she hugged her knees and listened to the trickling water. A slight breeze, hot and dry, stirred the air. A herd of longhorn cattle, maybe fifteen or twenty of them, drifted to the opposite side of the stream and began to drink, their wide horns knocking against one another as they huddled together. Their thirst slaked, the multicolored, lean cows began to low and to drift away.

They were beautiful. Mostly spotted, some were rust and white; tan-and-white hides marked the others. All had dark, solid lines down their powerful thews. Although she had lived all her life in Texas, Maureen had never been this close to the cattle that had put her home state on the map.

"Right pretty, aren't they?"

She started and turned to see her stepfather. "You half scared the pants off me, walking up quiet as an Indian!"

"Didn't mean to frighten you." Waving his finger at the cattle, Wilburn chuckled and sat down to share Maureen's makeshift rock chair. "Cade's done a lot with those cows."

"How so?"

"He's preserving the breed. The longhorns almost died out, you know, and if not for ranchers like my boy, they would be gone."

"I'll be darned." In the beginning, she had figured Cade for no more than a collector of designer cows, or seller to some sort of ritzy meat packer, if there were such a thing. His purpose with these cows added to his appeal. *Good gravy, Maureen, now you're liking him for his beef-on-the-hoof!*

"Enough about Cade." Wilburn tapped her hand. "You and I have something important to discuss. I bring good news. One of the Texas Bakeries big shots wants to hear more about Granny Miniver's Famous. I'm driving up to Dallas tonight."

"Who is the man?" she asked.

"Well, uh, um, can't recall off the top of my head. Must be getting senile," he added. His fingers withdrew from Maureen's and he patted his shirt pocket. "I've got his name written down. Must be in my other shirt."

"You haven't talked to anyone, have you?"

His face crumbled. "I've been trying, Sugar Pie, but it is the weekend. Figure if I turn up at Texas Bakeries come Monday morning, I'll get in to the executive suite. Then I'm heading out for Midland. Frank Bedichek's offered me a job selling drill pipe. Gotta get us some money, Sugar Pie."

"You don't need a job. You'll be in business yourself. Very soon." She blushed, realizing how much she had blurted. "I—I, uh, I agreed to go through with the sham engagement."

"I figured as much." Bones creaking, Wilburn turned away and shoved eight fingers into his back pockets. "Cade's lawyer got in contact with me this morning."

"His lawyer? You mean Cade didn't speak with you?"

"He told the fellow—right nice guy, mind you—everything he wanted got across."

What happened to the father-son parley? *Be patient.* Cade had made many strides, so she shouldn't expect too much at once. "You should talk with Cade. Just to make sure all the points are agreeable."

"No," he answered slowly. "I don't think so. I'm not wanting his *money,* Maureen."

Wilburn's misgivings wouldn't do, not at all. And if it took a guilt trip, so be it. "If you won't do it for yourself, do it for me. I've never minded having you around, and I've never begrudged a nickel I've spent on you, but I don't have a house to call my own, and the cookie factory is in trouble. Besides, it'll take weeks for you to see a paycheck."

"That's why I've gotta talk with the Texas Bakeries folks."

"Selling my name will take weeks, too." *If ever.*

"You're right." Wilburn gave an audible sigh and kicked a pebble into the creek. "But I hate to see you get into something you don't hanker for."

She moved to stand beside him. "I'm not complaining. Matter of fact, I'm looking forward to the next few weeks."

His eyes widened. *"What?"*

"You heard me. I want to be with Cade." She took a deep breath. "I want to know what makes him tick."

"You sweet on my boy?" Wilburn asked suspiciously. All of a sudden, his brown eyes danced. "That's it. You're sweet on him! Isn't that grand! My two kids together forever!"

"Not forever. Just for a few weeks."

"M'girl, you needn't be bashful with old Wilburn!" His eyes went soft. "Nothing would make me happier than to know my two kids . . . well, Cade needs a good woman like you, and you need a good man. Cade's a good man, you'll know that in time." Wilburn kissed her cheek. "And I'm gonna make you both a dad to be proud of. That bakery deal will be yours, and I'll turn a profit for my boy. Just you wait and see! We're going to be one happy family.

"I'm off to Dallas and points west," he continued. "You'll hear from me soon." A bounce in his step, Wilburn made for the house. "Everything'll be fine, you wait and see!"

She should have discouraged him, yet she hadn't wanted to dash the light in his eyes. But it was wrong to give him false hope.

Sunday arrived. The Smythe "cottage" at Canyon Lake was no mere lake cabin. It was a palatial two-story structure, built in the Spanish-colonial style, overlooking the green depths and craggy limestone shores of the man-made lake northeast of San Antonio.

The barbecue was held on a mammoth wooden patio adjoining the house, and it was well attended by guests, under beautiful, though scorching skies. A hundred prominent members of Texas's petroleum community enjoyed the country and western band, the groaning tables of pit-roasted meats and the libations tendered by servants uniformly decked out in string ties and ten-gallon hats. The air was redolent with scents beyond the food—flowers, lake air, the expensive perfumes of the guests. And as Cade had warned during the car trip to the lake, the guests made a big to-do over their "engagement."

Everyone wanted to know when the big day would be, but Cade said, "We haven't set a date."

By half past three, Sandra Uhr had not made an appearance, and Maureen dreaded her arrival. She and Cade were standing at the patio's edge, away from the dancers and next to a hedgerow of gardenias. What would she say to Sandra? Maureen worried. It would be easier...if they hadn't met at Cutter's Mill.

Cade leaned to whisper, "You're doing fine, Maureen. So fine I almost believed you, myself. You're a great actress."

"Somehow a 'thank-you' doesn't seem appropriate." Nervously, Maureen pushed a strand of hair from her temple. "Anyway, I'm worried about Sandra."

"Don't be. I spoke with her last night, and she took the news pretty well. All things considered."

"It's the all things considered that I'm worried about."

"Worrywart." Cade plucked a gardenia from one of the bushes, then tucked its stem behind her ear. "You look beautiful today." His gaze moved from her face to the fitted waist and full skirt of her off-the-shoulder Mexican dress. "Blue becomes you."

"You look pretty nice, yourself," she replied, meaning it and appreciating his compliment.

His forefinger touched the crocheted lace edge of her dress's gathered capelet as she looked over his apparel. He wore expensively cut Western attire, including a summer Stetson and handmade boots. As usual, he looked fantastic.

She cleared her throat. "From a suit to Yuppie attire to Western garb," she said, "you wear your clothes well."

Slowly, Cade's mouth moved into a smile. And the look in his eyes was pure satisfaction.

"Uh oh," she said. "Here comes Mr. Smythe." For the umpteenth time, she wound her arm through Cade's and waited for their host. "Lovely party. And Cade and I want to thank you for announcing our engagement," she said as coached.

"You're quite welcome." Douglas Smythe's face was pale beneath his tan. "I hope you young people will be happy. I wish you both every happiness." He managed a smile. "Be good to her, Cade. She's a nice gal."

"Rest assured, I'll take care of my darlin' here."

Douglas drilled a look into Cade's face. "See that you do." He receded into the crowd.

Maureen pulled her arm from Cade's. "I hate this," she whispered. "I don't like deceiving such a nice man."

Cade turned his back to the crowd and stood in front of Maureen. "I know Doug upset you, but don't let him. It'll take time for him to adjust, but he will. And think about this—how happy would he be if his daughter was in a loveless marriage?"

"Not too happy."

"Jake Patton," Cade muttered abruptly. Again he leaned to whisper. "Throw your arms around my neck. And kiss me. Now."

On tiptoe she lifted her hands to his nape and planted a closed-mouth smack on his lips. "How was that?" she asked.

"Unconvincing."

"Better you should teach me."

His eyes half-lidded, he drawled, "Better I should."

For a moment, she almost believed he wanted to teach her the fine art of kissing. A warm feeling eased through her. But she told herself not to make too much of his expression and tone. It was all for show. Why did that hurt?

"I understand best wishes and congratulations are in order," a voice boomed.

Cade stepped to Maureen's side, and she spied a balding giant. He looked to be at least fifty. And he must be seven feet tall, she thought in amazement as he flicked a cigar butt into the gardenia bushes.

"Maureen, this is Jake Patton. Jake, I'd like—"

The Goliath interrupted the introductions, and he talked to both of them at once. "So, you're the little gal who's gonna marry Cade here. Sure got yourself a looker, boy. 'Course you always did have a nose for blue-eyed brunets. So when's the big day, M'reen?" He hitched a thumb toward the refreshment bar. "Why don't you go fetch us a drink, Herrington? Make mine a triple Shirley Temple."

Darned if Cade didn't comply. Maureen was astounded that Cade Herrington, Midas of Texas petroleum, Saturday afternoon genie, would play step-and-fetch-it to anyone, much less to the overbearing Jake Patton.

"Ya met my wife yet?" Patton asked. "She's Pamela Bayard Patton, in case you didn't know, but I'm sure you do."

Am I supposed to be impressed? "I don't believe I've had the honor, but there are a lot of people here today."

"Oh, you'd remember my Pammie. I'm surprised Herrington hasn't introduced you, seeing as how they used to be engaged. 'Fore I stole her away, that is."

Cade had been engaged? And this pompous oaf had stolen her away? Surely not. Never once had Wilburn mentioned Cade having plans for marriage, and hadn't Cade said he wasn't the forever kind? This man had to be kidding, because no woman in her right mind would choose Jake Patton over Cade Herrington.

"Whussa matter, M'reen? Seen a ghost?"

"My feet are hurting," she lied. "That's all."

"Pam can wear five-inch heels for hours, and her dogs never bark. That's her over there." He pointed a sausage-like finger in the direction of the bandstand. "She's the good-looking brunet yammering with that shrimp of a fellow."

"She is lovely," Maureen said truthfully.

Patton grabbed Maureen's arm and hauled her toward the bandstand. Booming as usual and draping an arm around his wife's shoulders, he made introductions.

"You're getting a great guy," Pamela said, no trace of regret in her voice as she smiled up into her husband's marshmallow-and-mashed-potato face. "I thought Cade was the most wonderful man alive. Until I met Jake."

Apparently Jake had hidden talents, or the Patton brand of baloney extended to his wife. *Why are you being so nasty about the Pattons?* she asked herself. Well, Maureen could criticize Cade, but she didn't want anyone else either making a monkey out of him or comparing him unfavorably to a loud-mouthed boor.

Somewhat curious, Maureen asked Pamela, "How long have you been married?"

Jake's gargantuan chest swelled with pride as he did the answering. "Going on thirteen years. Got four younguns, too."

Right then, a bandy-legged man demanded a "whirl through the sawdust with the bride," and Maureen was grateful to take leave of giant and wife. By the time the waltz ended, another man asked for a turn. Then another and another and another. She listened to their jokes and stories, laughing along.

Halfway through a Texas two-step, Cade tapped her partner on the shoulder. "I'm cutting in."

Cade whirled her into his arms. He was a marvelous dancer, light on his feet and in tune with the music. She felt his hand at the small of her back, smelled the woodsy scent of his after-shave . . . and caught the daggers in his eyes.

"You've been flirting," he charged, the music giving privacy. "That's not acceptable behavior for an engaged woman."

"Listen here, that's what you get for abandoning me to Jake Patton. And for not telling me you'd been engaged to his wife."

"Quite frankly, I don't think about Pam along those lines. She and I were a long, long time ago."

For some odd reason, Maureen believed him. Yet . . . there had to be some basis for his bitterness. She had no time to mull her thoughts, not with Cade pulling her closer, his breath feathering her ear as he stopped dancing.

"We'd better do something to convince the bystanders I'm the man for you."

One palm still at her back, he moved the other to cup her jaw . . . and his mouth slanted across hers. It was as if a thousand prisms of awareness planed through her head, her limbs, her heart. His lips, tasting of champagne, were conquering, and no urge to pull away possessed her. She melted into his embrace. He groaned, and his kiss deepened and explored. He wasn't acting, she thought wildly. He couldn't be! No one could put this much passion into make-believe.

Her heart pounding, she tangled her fingers into his rich black hair. Right then she knew . . . she accepted the truth. She didn't despise him—and never had. Despite her past anger at Cade, she had never stopped finding him attractive. From the first time she had laid eyes on him, when she was but a girl, she had wanted to be caught in his arms. She had been lying to herself for a long time.

Too soon, he pulled away. "Now you've had a teacher." His lips feathered her eyelid. With sternness in his inflection, he demanded, "Don't forget the lesson."

The magic spell broken, she excused herself and turned away from Cade. She needed to gather her thoughts.

Less than a minute later, she descended the thirty steps to the lake and walked onto the long dock. An egret dove for its dinner while water lapped at the pilings, and Maureen inhaled the fish-scented air. Brushing an errant strand of hair from her cheek as the summer sun kissed her exposed shoulders, she sat down on a wooden bench and fell to thought. What was she going to do, now that she accepted her attraction to Cade? Soon their time together would be over, and she'd go back to being the baker from west San Antonio and he'd go back to being the playboy tycoon. She needed to distance her emotions. But how easy would that be?

She heard footsteps. Cade? No, it couldn't be him, the footfalls were too light. Maureen turned to the side, and her heart jumped into her throat. Sandra Smythe Uhr was approaching.

Hurt and anger in her eyes, the petite blonde bit out, "Why didn't you tell me about you and Cade?"

Chapter Five

As Sandra glided down the boat dock below her father's lake palace, Maureen took a deep breath. This was the moment she had dreaded all afternoon. Beyond her anxiety, she had to convince the blonde that the engagement was "true." If she didn't, she would be letting Cade down, which was now unthinkable.

"Out at Cutter's Mill, why didn't you tell me about you and Cade?" Sandra repeated, her words mingling with the sounds from the barbecue.

Maureen waited for a noisy motorboat to pass before she answered, "I had no idea who you were."

"Is that so? You had no idea Cade owned that particular piece of property. And you were in the dark about me. You really keep abreast of your fiancé's interests." Petulant and with less than her usual grace, Sandra plopped down on the wooden bench. "I find it very hard to believe Cade would fall in love and propose marriage to a woman he barely knows."

"Cade and I do know each other quite well. We've known each other for years. I'll admit it's been only recently that the two of us have fallen in love." Maureen almost stumbled over "love," but thankfully Sandra didn't notice. "But does it matter how long we've been seeing each other? We know we want to spend the rest of our lives together."

"I thought he felt that way about me." The wealthy girl's chin trembled. "Instead, he was just out to get rid of, of..."

"He didn't, and doesn't, want to hurt you, Sandra—neither of us do," she said earnestly.

"You have." Sandra's face was a mask of pain. "I feel so empty, so lost. I just don't know what to do."

Maureen's heart ached for her. And guilt was a palpable thing. This lying business was awful! "You have so many options. You could travel or get a job or talk with your hus—"

"I can't do any of that!" Frustration replaced the self-pity in Sandra's delicate features. "Right now I can't think of anything but how strange this engagement of yours is. There's never been a whisper that you and Cade were involved. And when I need him most, he turns to you.

"Here you are, sharing a mutual father, but where is the man? Nowhere to be seen on one of the biggest days of your lives—the afternoon your engagement is announced."

There were weaknesses in this plan of Cade's, but she had to be convincing. "He's away on business. He'd be here if he could."

"If my father put his priorities on business rather than being with me at my engagement party, I'd never speak to him again." The blonde wrinkled her aristocratic nose. "This whole situation smells as fishy as this lake air."

Maureen looked away, across the water. Was there a chance of switching the topic? She turned her regard back to the other woman. "I'd like to say something. Do you mind if I'm blunt?"

"If it'll help me understand, do go on."

"You don't really love Cade, I know you don't." *Please let this work.* "I feel certain you still love your husband."

Sandra's mouth dropped, but she closed it and unbowed her spine. "You've been listening to Cade. He's made up his mind that way to ease his conscience over me." She shook her head. "Believe me, I—I don't l-love Phil. He and I are through. Cade is . . . was the man for me."

"What Cade said about you has no bearing on my remark. You and I had a pretty frank talk that day at Cutter's Mill, and I knew then that you're still in love with your husband. Why don't you try to patch things up?"

"Advice from you is the last thing I want." Sandra jumped to her feet and hugged her arms. Her big gray eyes focused on Maureen, and she asked, "The question is, do you *really* love Cade?"

Attracted to him, Maureen was. Frequently she found him infuriating. He could be cold and calculating. But at other times, she had cracked his reserve to find him infinitely appealing. He fascinated her. She yearned to know about his past, to understand the pain that etched his soul. Perhaps she was a little bit in love with him. "Of course I do."

A tear trickled down Sandra's cheek. "Be good to him, then. He's been awfully special to me and my father for an awfully long time, and if anyone ever hurt him... Don't ever hurt him, Maureen! Please don't. He had enough of that from Pam."

Maureen tensed, yet a burst of understanding shot through her brain. Pamela Patton had been the one. She'd turned him bitter! A thousand questions screamed to be verbalized, but she wouldn't ask them, not in front of Sandra. They were questions any engaged woman *should* know about her intended.

"I won't hurt Cade," Maureen said honestly. "I promise you that."

For a long moment, Sandra studied her expression. "Then you have my best wishes, Maureen." She ascended the steps leading up to the barbecue.

Maureen gave thanks that Sandra was somewhat appeased.

A week passed. After the barbecue, Cade had offered a lift to a friend whose ranch bordered on the Dry Hole, and his and Maureen's conversation afterward had been limited to Sandra's reaction. He had left Maureen at the ranch's front door, and not once had she heard from him since.

Wilburn, however, had returned this morning. She caught a trace of uncertainty in him, though he tried to mask it. Nothing was settled with Texas Bakeries. They were "taking it under advisement." This wasn't positive news. Naturally Maureen was disappointed, but Wilburn would not throw in the towel.

Her stepfather was somewhat of a help with the mystery of Cade, though. He told her his son and Pamela had been college sweethearts, but the woman quit school to marry the chief executive officer of Patton Petroleum. It wasn't much for Maureen to go on.

Right now, on Sunday afternoon, she sat in the stark-white kitchen that would be any cook's dream. While the cookies were baking, Maureen made entries in her bookkeeping journals. In addition to notations for Granny Miniver's Famous, she was keeping careful records of all monies owed to Cade.

From the corner of her eye, she saw him approach. And in the aftermath of promising herself to keep her emotions intact, she steeled herself against his presence.

She grabbed her checkbook and began to write. Flourishing the finished product, she said proudly, "Here's the first installment on my loan."

"You don't need to—" Evidently he caught the determined pride in her bearing, for he eyed the amount. "Hmm. Looks like Granny Miniver's doing well."

"Ted's done a fine job of placing the product in new markets. And I've collected on some receivables I never imagined would be paid."

"Heard anything on your insurance settlement?"

She shook her head. "Not a word. The insurance company is still investigating." The evening she and Wilburn had moved to the ranch, Cade had accused his father of being culpable in the fire. Mentioning now that Al Assurers tended to blame him, too, would open a can of worms. Maureen had no wish to soil the conversation with squiggling things. "I'm sure the settlement will come through any day."

He studied her. "Sandra went to dinner last night with Phil," he announced as he helped himself to a double handful of chocolate-chip cookies. "Mmm, these are delicious," he murmured.

"I'm happy to hear that, on both counts." She placed the pen aside. "Cade...your father is here at the ranch."

"I know."

"Have you...have you talked with him?"

"I have. On the telephone." Cade brushed crumbs from his hand. "Matter of fact, you'll be happy to know I've set up an appointment with him for later this afternoon. That's why I'm here. And I'd like for you to sit in on the meeting, so you'll know I'm living up to my end of the deal."

Although relieved that he was making an effort, Maureen was wrought with sudden frustration. "A Sunday afternoon meeting wasn't what I had in mind, Cade. You *promised* to spend a weekend with him. Just the two of you."

"I haven't forgotten anything. But I won't be pushed, dammit. When Wilburn and I have our little powwow, it'll be in my own good time. For right now, it's strictly business. Understand?"

She had been pushing. While she yearned for a quick settlement between the two Herringtons, she forced an, "I understand."

"Good." Cade swiped another cookie and switched the subject again. "Don't make plans for the Fourth of July. I'm hosting a dinner party at my penthouse, and I expect you to be the hostess. It'll be black tie, so dress accordingly. Would you like to know the guest list?"

"Sure."

"Sandra and Doug, of course. I've invited Phil, too. And the Pattons will be there."

"The Pattons? Why invite them?" Maureen frowned. "Why would you invite your ex-fiancée?" she asked boldly.

"I didn't invite Pam. I invited *Jake* and his wife."

"Well, I'm certainly in a quandary now," Maureen said crossly. "That man is god-awful."

"I'm not asking you to like him, I'm telling you to be his hostess."

Maureen ground her teeth. "Why is he important to you?"

"He's an influential board member of the Petroleum Producers Association. I'm running for president, and I need Jake's support."

"One member of the board shouldn't make such a difference in an organization as large as the PPA, so why do you feel it's necessary to be in company with him?"

"Haven't you ever heard of associating with your peers?"

"Of course I have, but I don't think anything would be important enough to force me to endure the company of that oaf."

"That's where you and I differ. I'll do anything or be around anybody who'll help me win that presidency."

She was startled by the ruthlessness and vehemence in Cade's tone. There were so many things she didn't know about the man she was supposed to "wed." "How could a mere elected post be that coveted?"

"It'll show Texas that the Herrington name isn't a joke."

"Excuse me?"

Cade, his arms akimbo, his head lowered, paced the terrazzo floor. When he stopped, he fastened his troubled gaze on Maureen, and his words were pained. "My father was running for the PPA presidency when he and my mother divorced. He was soundly defeated. And I don't have to tell you what a muck he made of himself after that. When I got into this business, no one wanted to take me seriously. If not for Doug, I would've never gotten a chance to prove myself."

"But you've done that."

"Not really. I won't be satisfied until I've achieved what my father could not."

His ambition had nothing to do with proving something to the Texas oil community, she surmised. Cade—for himself—needed to gain one-upmanship over Wilburn. Oh, Lord. This was one bitter man. She stood and covered the distance between them, then looked into his eyes, her heart doing a double beat. "You resent your father because he wasn't able to do for you. That's the problem, isn't it?"

"No," he answered earnestly. "Maureen, all I wanted was to be proud of him."

This was the first inkling of a resolution to her goal, and delight wound through every cell in her being.

"He'll make you proud." Right now, though, nothing was settled, and she touched Cade's square jaw. "I'm sorry you've been hurt."

He laughed and pulled her close. "I'm not looking for pity, I'm just trying to stop your infernal questions."

Her nose was against the clean, herbal scent of his shirt, and she reveled in the warmth of Cade's body. It was wicked how her fingers *just happened* to brush the chest hair exposed above his shirt buttons.

His palm pressed against those fingers, and she jumped back. In a dither, she asked the first thing unrelated to Cade that came to mind. "Don't you think Jake's a real reprobate?"

"Yeah." Cade laughed and to her relief didn't make a deal out of her aggressiveness. He poured a cup of coffee, scooted a chair from the table and sat down. She did the same. He took a swallow of the steaming brew, then said, "He's a scalawag, all right."

"Tell me about him."

"Jake is my most vocal adversary in the PPA. Always has been." Cade took a sip of coffee. "The ole boy's insecure. He's a big, ugly, hulking buffoon, and he knows it. But he doesn't crawl into some hole and lick his wounds—he goes for the throat of anyone who crosses him. Fortunately for Jake, he has money backing him. Any time he can grab something that someone else has, he gloats. Such was the case with Pam. He got her, so he gloats. And he's jealous of me, because he thinks I could steal her...if I wanted to."

"Do you want to? Steal her away, that is." Maureen waited with bated breath.

"Never in a million years." Cade shook his head. "She's not the woman I fell in love with. *If* I ever did love her."

Maureen sighed in relief. "I can't imagine why she picked him instead of you."

A grin waved over Cade's face. "You're blushing, Maureen.... I like it when you do that." He reached across the table to touch her jawline. "I've got an idea.... When we're with others, why don't you think about something that'll make you blush? Look at me when you do it. That way everyone will think you're having lascivious thoughts about...say, our wedding night."

Fiery blood coursed into Maureen's face, the likes of which she had never experienced before. "W-wedding night?"

"That was hypothetical." His eyes were half-lidded. "I'll admit I've thought about taking you to bed. Well, you're very beautiful, and I've taken a few cold showers, thinking about...the way you, uh, look."

Maureen cleared her throat and endeavored to still her rampant emotions. Recalling her stepfather's tales of Cade's many women was a help. "You've done a lot of that, haven't you? Slept with women you don't care about."

"I don't kiss and tell, Maureen. Besides, I'd rather talk about you and me...and putting an end to those showers."

She tugged her hand from the fingers that were now tracing the side of her palm. "Sex and sex talk aren't part of our arrangement."

"We could renegotiate the terms."

"Not on your life."

"Hardheaded woman." He chuckled, then sniffed. "Smells like something's burning."

Something was burning. Her desire. She wondered what it would be like to be in Cade's bed—she'd never been in any man's bed. She went for the charred cookies. How in the heck was she going to keep her heart in check? Here she was, after the first face-to-face she'd had with Cade since her decision not to let him affect her, and she had blushed and blushed and blushed . . . all the while responding to the man who just wanted relief from icy water. And a partner in his scheme.

He strode out of the kitchen, calling over his shoulder. "Meeting's in ten minutes. Don't be late."

On time as Cade had demanded, Maureen entered the den where he and Wilburn were waiting. As if there were an invisible wall between them, they stood on opposite sides of the room. She sat on the cordovan sofa; Cade took an oversize chair. His father continued to stand.

Cade settled his elbows on the armrests, steepled his fingers. "What plans have you got for the money I gave you?"

Wilburn licked his lips. "I, uh, I, um—I suppose I'll get back in the couplings business."

"You *suppose?* You've had time to get your act together, so why are you still at the supposing stage?"

"Well, you know how it is, son. I've gotta look into all the opportunities."

Maureen prompted, "Didn't you tell me you'd done a feasibility study into—"

"Pencil pushers do feasibility studies, Maureen, not on-line men," Cade cut in. "What's your gut feeling?" he asked Wilburn.

"West Texas needs another couplings supplier like a hog needs a sidesaddle. New fittings cost too much for the average drilling contractor. They need an affordable alternative."

A faint light of respect flickered in Cade's eyes, and Maureen's hopes rose. "You're right," he said. "So where does that leave you?"

"To be honest, son, I don't know."

Oh, no! Why didn't you show him your stuff! Of course, Maureen couldn't say those words, and no one else spoke, either. The tick of the grandfather clock was the only noise, and the sound seemed as loud as Big Ben.

Finally, Cade spoke. "Wash 'em."

"Do what?" Wilburn asked, astonishment in his weathered features.

"Wash old couplings and resell them."

"By doggies, that's a smart idea! Why, ever'body'll be after 'em. It'll save drillers thousands of dollars. Millions of dollars!"

Cade frowned. "Don't let high-flying ideas go to your head. We're talking experiment."

"You . . . you're right, son."

Cade got to his feet, reaching for a long roll of paper that he handed to his father. "This is a plan for another experiment, something I've been working on awhile. I don't know if it'll work, but if I've done my engineering right, this machine will put old, out-of-round fittings back to industry specifications."

Wilburn perused the blueprints with Maureen looking over his shoulder. She wasn't an engineer and knew nothing about machinery, but she knew oil-field couplings were rather like colossal nuts connecting lengths of thirty-foot drill pipe, thus making as much as several thousand feet of continuous steel pipe to sink drilling bits down exploration wells. Would this crazy-looking machine work? she wondered. Of course it would. The fingers of Midas had touched it; it was Cade's design.

His eyes widening as he looked up at his son, Wilburn said, "It'll work, my boy. It'll work."

"Just like everything in life, the proof is in the doing. Prove yourself, Wilburn Herrington."

"I will."

Imparting a half look Maureen's way, Cade demanded, "Find something to do. I want a private word with my father."

Irritated that she had been summarily dismissed, but pleased that Cade had spoken the words "my father"—not to mention the implied trust of those blueprints—she retired to the kitchen.

By the time Cade joined her there, her joy knew no bounds. Everything was going to be wonderful in the Herrington family.

She handed him a plate of cookies and a mug of coffee. "Thanks for going above and beyond the call of our partnership, giving him those blueprints."

"I was protecting my investment. Handing the old man fifty thou just to squander was never my intention."

"He wouldn't have squandered it."

"Your faith is blind, sweetheart."

"If you don't trust him, just a little, why did you give him plans for a valuable piece of machinery?"

"I gave him nothing. The machine is still mine. All I gave him was a *copy* of my idea and a few weeks to see if he can get it going. If he fails, all I've lost is time. And I've gained... Well, he'll keep busy, either figuring out a way to stall on finding a machinist, or—" Cade grimaced.

Was it only a moment ago that she was filled with hope? Even though Cade had entrusted his invention to Wilburn, he was the same bitter and distrusting soul.

"He won't let you down. I trust him implicitly."

Should she tell him about Wilburn's plan to sell Granny Miniver's Famous to Texas Bakeries? Probably not. The idea had the earmarks of a dreamer's folly—not the impression she wanted to give Cade.

"You'll trust him, too," she added. "Soon. I know you will, and if there's anything I can do to help the two of you, I'll do it."

"Don't set yourself up as a modern-day Joan of Arc, trying to save the tatters of the Herrington family. It's too late for that. We're beyond saving."

"I don't agree. I know your father wants to reconcile. And, Cade, I'm beginning to know you. You're bitter over something, maybe several things, and I hate for you to hurt."

He took a step forward. "You're seeing matters through the eyes of a sentimental woman. Not with realism. I told you once not to concern yourself with my welfare, and I meant it. I'm a big boy, Maureen, and I fight my own battles."

"This isn't a battle, it's a family affair. I am a part of the Herrington family, not some martyr at the stake, and I don't deserve to be kept in the dark about this problem you have with your father."

"Why don't you ask him about it? Ask him, Maureen. Make him tell you the truth."

"All right, I take the challenge. I *will* find out the problem, and *right now!*" She started across the kitchen floor, but Cade's next words stopped her.

"Impossible. He left."

"Left? Where did he go?"

"Off to chase his windmills."

"But," she sputtered, "he wouldn't leave without telling me goodbye."

"He did because I told him to. I told him to leave you the hell alone."

"You did *what?*"

"I told him to get gone and stay gone. You don't need him hanging around, playing on your soft heart."

"Don't you think that was for me to decide?"

"Not in this incident," Cade answered coldly. "I've got to protect my investment in you. Sandra's not back with Phil, you know, and I won't have your thoughts muddied with Wilburn Herrington."

Furious, Maureen parked her hands on her hips. "You don't own me. And I resent your interference in my life."

In an economy of motions, Cade strode over to stand in front of her. Leaning to stare into her eyes, he ground out, "You want to interfere in mine. Why shouldn't I interfere in yours?"

His lips took hers then, cutting off her comeback. The fire of emotion went into his kiss. His hands were like molten lava as he caressed her shoulders, her back, her derriere. His tongue touched hers, and his was sweet as hot chocolate. She melted.

But somehow she found her wits. Aggravating, contrary, irritating man! How dare he exile her beloved Wilburn, then, like some caveman, yank her into his arms for a kiss?

Sure, he wanted to relieve his sexual urges, but where would that lead? Into an unacceptable situation.

Pulling away, she dragged in a lungful of air that eased, somewhat, the pounding of blood in her heart...her limbs...her ears. Wordlessly she whipped around, leaving him in the kitchen.

Her bedroom door slammed behind her, and she dropped onto the window seat and realized she had wanted to savor Cade's kiss.

"You," she grumbled, "are in deep trouble."

Her eyes cut to the right. Through the window she spied Cade atop a large black horse, riding hell for leather toward the hills. Riding like a man besieged with trouble. Surely their latest argument wasn't the source. Heated words were the norm between them.

What was Cade's problem?

Chapter Six

Riding into the hot, afternoon wind and away from Maureen and their most recent clash of wills, Cade stewed over his dilemma. How in the hell had he allowed this situation to get out of control?

For more than an hour, he pushed Titan to the limit of endurance, and what did he gain? Nothing. Nothing but a winded black stallion.

Irritated with himself for abusing horseflesh, Cade headed back to the stable and waved away the groom's assistance. "Make yourself scarce," he told the young man. Cade stomped across the hay-strewn planking, gathered the sweat rug and threw it across the stallion's back.

"It's a sad day when a man takes his frustrations out on an animal," he said, filling the trough with fresh water and going for the body brush. "It's a sad day when a man loses control of himself. I've done a lot of that lately." He ran his palm down Titan's damp forehead. "I shouldn't have kissed

Maureen. Not like I did, anyway. Grabbing her, showing my anger. My weakness."

Not being prone to heart-to-heart chats with horses—and with his usual confidant, Douglas, being the last person he could call on in this instance—Cade grimaced and set to cooling down the lathered stallion. The task occupied his hands, but not his thoughts.

Both he and Maureen were guilty of interfering in each other's lives. There was no denying that. Meddling in the Herrington family rift was as familiar as cookies to Maureen, even though Cade wanted her to stay out of the mess. For her own sake. Enough people had been hurt by Wilburn's unprincipled, undisciplined ways.

Yes, he had been cross with Maureen, but now that he had time to think about it, he realized he had been transferring anger. He was mad as hell at his father.

When this afternoon's meeting had begun, he hadn't been angry. Matter of fact, he'd had a grudging respect for Wilburn's honesty and interest. Of course that openness and enthusiasm had dissipated the moment Maureen had left the den. Cade hadn't been surprised. But he had been disappointed, angry—if not furious!—when Wilburn didn't put up any argument at being sent away.

Cade yanked the sweat rug from Titan's back and began to comb the black hide. "Damn him. After all the trouble Maureen had gone to, helping him, he doesn't seem to give a care about her welfare. Not like I do. For all that old goat knows, she and I could be shacking up together. You'd think he'd have some fatherly concern."

Titan snorted. The arch look he cast his master's way seemed to ask, "And where have you been burying your head, Herrington? You ought to know better than to expect his integrity."

Cade swallowed a nasty, tinny taste. Wilburn was a no-good. Nothing more, nothing less.

So, what did that make him—a son unable to respect the commandment, "Honor thy father"? There were no qualifications attached to that edict. It was simply, honor thy father. Impossible. Cade was too bitter and cynical for it. He knew it, didn't try to deny it. Even to himself. Life had turned him that way.

First hand, he knew the heartache Wilburn had wreaked on the first Mrs. Herrington. In her hurt and anger over her husband's illicit affair with his secretary, Rowena had offered him a sizable settlement for a divorce. All it took was one heated challenge and Wilburn, without so much as an argument for appearance's sake, had cleaned out the bank accounts.

Cade should have learned his lesson from that. But he hadn't. Gullible as a sucker in a shell game, he allowed himself to be taken in by Pamela. When she dumped him for Jake's fat pocketbook, Cade gave up trusting anyone. He became certain that anyone would sell his soul to the devil, if the offer was high enough.

And that included Maureen.

When he suggested their engagement charade, Cade had figured everyone involved had something to gain. Sandra could repair her marriage; Maureen would get whatever she wanted, be it for herself or for Wilburn. As for Cade, it didn't hurt, his having a "fiancée" to impress the conservatives at the PPA.

Things had changed for him the night Maureen's hovel caught fire. The moment he observed the helplessness and despair in her big lapis-lazuli eyes, he had been determined to protect her. Since then, he had done everything in his power to please her. By entrusting those blueprints to Wilburn, Cade had gotten what he set out to accomplish:

Maureen's delight. Her smile, the light in her eyes, her pleasure—these had been worth a million new inventions.

Frowning, he put away the grooming supplies and began to fill oat buckets for all twelve of his horses. *Herrington, you're doing it again. You're letting a woman get under your skin. You're asking for trouble.*

What exactly did he want from Maureen? To be more than a moneybags stepbrother. He wanted her to run into his arms and savor his kisses. For her to initiate an embrace or two.

Maybe her reluctance had to do with innocence. Cade hadn't a doubt about her purity, even though she was a child by no means. As for himself, he hadn't been a virgin since Sally May Klein had invited him to her mama's house to drink cherry colas and "play records." That had been many moons ago.

Thirty-four seemed old right now, compared to a fresh almost-twenty-four. Old, hell. He was experienced, that was all. Skilled enough to introduce Maureen to the finer points of lovemaking.

To get to that stage, however, she needed to notice Cade Herrington as a man. What would it take? Buying her attention had been somewhat successful. What could he give her that would guarantee her attention?

Herrington, use a little common sense. You're not bald, fat and toothless. Make yourself available... but not too much so.

He quit the stable and strode to the house, where he found Maureen seated in the den, the blinds closed. She looked so beautiful, curled up in his oversize chair. Her eyes, big and beguiling, stared up at him. With a trembling hand, she brushed a strand of dark hair from her temple as she shuttered those eyes. Though she was tall and not tiny by any stretch of the imagination, she seemed little and vulnerable and helpless.

He yearned to crouch at her feet, apologize for yelling at her, maybe ask for a kiss of reconciliation. But he didn't.

He poured himself a shot of whiskey, downed it and announced before making an exit, "I'll be staying here at the ranch from here on out."

Amazed at Cade's announcement, Maureen dropped her jaw and stared at his departing form. The least he could have done was apologize for sending Wilburn away. Or for acting like a caveman, yanking her into that kiss. Or for—

For what? *Be honest, Maureen.* Just as he had charged earlier today, she had been interfering in his life. Maybe she should be apologizing to him.

Baloney. By the following morning, though, she was prepared to apologize, or whatever it took to make peace. Why, she didn't quite understand. But surely it had to do with her appreciation for all Cade had done, both for Wilburn and for her.

But she'd give him the first opportunity to apologize.

The housekeeper, Frieda Wittig, was more than agreeable in allowing Maureen to prepare breakfast. So, Maureen set about making a western omelette, oat bran muffins and link sausages. Decaffeinated coffee—the imported kind that cost an arm and a leg—hummed through the drip-o-lator. She whistled a Pointer Sisters' tune while pouring hot cream into a pitcher.

A big hairy hand reaching for the cookie jar caused her to jump—right back against a solid wall of silk-covered brawn. Before she could do something stupid, like purr and arch her cheek against the scent of soapy clean man, Maureen eyed Cade and gushed, "Wow, you look great in a kimono."

"Izzat so?" he drawled, taking a long gander at her scarlet face.

She recovered aplomb and replied, "That's so."

Actually, he looked great, period. In the past, he had been impeccably dressed, but today was a different story. Tousled hair. A morning beard darkening his jaw—if he had showered, why hadn't he shaved? The silk kimono was loosened at the chest to reveal tufts of chest curls matching the raven's-wing black of his hair. She liked the way he looked, first thing in the morning. It was as if he had a certain vulnerability. He had never looked so handsome.

"Look, Maureen, about yesterday, I didn't set out to yell at you. Or to kiss you. Can we put it in the past and get on with our plans?"

"Uh, yeah. Sure."

Right now she was too rattled by his presence to make an intelligent reply. She didn't know what she wanted. And quite honestly, she couldn't recall what they needed to put in the past. The drool-swoons had hit her.

A handful of cookies in his fist, he turned and walked toward the kitchen table. He flexed his shoulder muscles, as if he had a crick in his neck. She hankered to move closer and massage away his discomfort. But she didn't. And her gaze lowered.

For some odd reason, Maureen couldn't take her eyes from Cade's legs. Reaching three inches above his knees, the kimono might have displayed knobby joints and grainy calf muscles. In this case, Michelangelo's David never looked so good.

Swallowing, Maureen watched Cade bend to sit. The midnight-blue robe gapped open as he did so. She whipped her face back to the cream pitcher but not before catching a glimpse of hairy thighs and red briefs. Very brief red briefs.

"Ah, um, w-would you... Breakfast is red. I—I mean ready."

"These cookies are enough for me, thank you." He bit into one, then reached for the *Wall Street Journal*. "Where's Frieda?"

"Doing the laundry." Maureen parked her hands on her hips. "Don't you want to try the breakfast I cooked for you?"

Was that a grin he swallowed? "It does smell good," he allowed.

Pleased, Maureen twirled around, intent on serving the meal. In doing so, her eyes caught Cade's. And there was something infinitely arresting in his expression.

Alas, his interest waned. He hid behind the newspaper and said nary another word for the remainder of the meal.

That set the pattern for the next week. She prepared breakfast, and he devoured the fare. But he was cool and detached. Of course his demeanor changed when they were in company with his associates, which was every evening. Then, he was lovey-dovey, kissy-huggy. But as soon as they arrived back at the Dry Hole, he became impersonal, inaccessible, infuriating.

His actions had a marked effect on Maureen. She didn't know what to think or what to do, but decided to give what she got: the icy treatment.

By the time that week had passed, she had had just about enough. She wanted his attention, by darn! To heck with cool.

To alleviate frustrations, she decided exercise would do her good. Recalling Cade's offer, that she could make use of his horses, she decided a ride in the cool evening air would clear her chaotic mind. She dressed in jeans and a pullover shirt before walking to the stable to select a palomino mare, Sadie. Not ten minutes into the ride, she spied another rider.

Cade.

Should she turn around? Or should she take a deep breath and ride forward?

Under a cloudless and starlit sky, Cade's black stallion pranced over the Dry Hole's familiar terrain. A midnight ride usually cured what ailed Titan's master, or at least relaxed Cade, but tonight? No way. His plan, Operation Notice Me, had boomeranged. Over the past week, he had noticed Maureen, and noticed her and noticed her. And noticed her. Though he had tried to be sly about it. While he could claim a modicum of success in the game—she had paid some attention to Cade—he wouldn't count himself the victor.

The sound of horse hooves caused Cade to look to the right. His pulse raced, a grin cutting across his face. "Well, whaddya know..." Maureen was headed his way.

Cade might win this game after all.

He ordered, "Whoa, boy," and waited.

She rode abreast of his mount, reined in the mare. "Fancy meeting you here," she said somewhat nervously.

Elated at her presence and driven by his wild passions, Cade relished the sound of her voice. He wanted her, needed her... What would she do if he grabbed her out of that saddle, and...? *Get serious, Herrington.*

She spoke again. "Nice evening for a ride."

Cade grinned and tried to deny the libidinous heat building in him. He'd had a lot of practice along that line, lately. Maybe he could quit ignoring his needs—soon. She had, after all, been the aggressor in this meeting.

She reached from her saddle to stroke Titan's generous mane. "Beautiful horse you've got here, Cade."

"I'm an admirer of all things primo," he replied, taking a sneaky look at the someone most primo. Thank God for moonless nights and Maureen's attention to Titan, he could take a long drink of her wealth of rich sable hair and the shapely figure wreaking havoc on all sorts of his places—without making too much of a slavering fool of himself.

"Sadie's a nice horse, too," Maureen pointed out, giving the prized palomino a stroke on the neck and missing the point of Cade's statement. "What got you interested in horses?"

These were two of the many things Cade admired about Maureen. Inquisitiveness and innocence. Innocence that was sometimes too inquisitive and astute for his comfort. Curiosity that made her interested and interesting.

"A guy can't have a ranch without horses," he replied to her latest question. "Speaking of which, let's ride." He headed Titan toward a stretch of cleared land, and Maureen guided the mare to his side. "Strength and power, that's a horse," he commented. "It didn't take me long to learn to love them."

Love, he thought. Interesting word. He feared he was falling in love with Maureen. Maybe he had been in love since the moment she charged into his office.

Maureen seemed to epitomize everything he could want in a woman. He admired her. She was the type of person who'd go bear hunting with a switch. She worked like a section hand to get her cookie factory back on line. She held her own with his acquaintances, and he was proud to show her off to his friends and associates. Considerate and kind—these adjectives fit her, too. While Cade wanted nothing to do with his father, he admired Maureen's unflagging loyalty to him. None of which held a candle to his obsession with the irritating, inquisitive, opinionated, utterly beguiling Maureen Miniver. *Awful last name. Much too severe for her. I could change it.*

He wasn't falling in love with Maureen. He was in love with her. These astounding realizations nearly knocked him out of his custom-made saddle.

"Are you all right, Cade?" She reached for his arm, and her touch was tender yet sure. "Cade?"

"I'm fine."

Finer than he had been in a long time. Or was he? A fist knotted in his chest. He wanted to believe Maureen was all he wanted her to be.

Surely she was different from the rest, and wasn't out for number one, but he couldn't ignore a blatant recollection. Before she agreed to the engagement bit, Maureen had demanded—not asked for, but *demanded!*—the option to Cutter's Mill.

He didn't begrudge the land and gristmill. A gold platter wouldn't be good enough to hold the deed as he handed it to her...provided he'd done the offering. What the hell? He owned real estate from here to everywhere, so two measly acres and an old building had nothing to do with Cade's hesitation. The principle of the thing stood between them.

He wanted a wife who didn't have a price tag. Yet there was a weakness to his will that yearned to disregard doubts and give her—give them both—a chance. If he could be certain of her, he'd marry her in a New York minute.

"We're moving too fast," he mumbled.

"Why, Cade, we're not! These horses are standing still as posts."

There she went again, being the innocent. He threw back his head and laughed. The saddle creaked as he leaned to kiss her cheek. "Let's get back on the path."

Their relationship was whizzing along, way too fast. It was time to ease back.

Cade needed to know that Maureen could be trusted. Becoming lovers had been utmost in his thoughts, but he decided that might not be the best tack. If Maureen proved she was trustworthy, he didn't want to spoil their wedding night. If she wasn't trustworthy, he had no desire to get tangled in a sticky situation.

A sticky situation. Now that he had come to grips with his emotions, Cade faced a problem. He hadn't been totally aboveboard with Maureen about his motivation for the so-called engagement. He was no prototype for character superexcellence, and if it turned out she was, what would she say about his motives?

She cut into his concerns with, "You're quiet tonight."

"I've got a lot on my mind."

As if Maureen didn't have enough on her mind, wedding presents began to arrive, even though no date had been set for the "nuptials." Apparently word had spread fast on the heels of Douglas Smythe's barbecue. Daily, the Rolls Royce from San Antonio's finest shop halted at the front door to deposit gift after gift after gift. The givers? Cade's acquaintances. Maureen didn't open the boxes, but foresaw weeks of laborious attention to notes of explanation upon their return. She had never felt so awful about the engagement's elaborate ruse. Good people had gone to trouble and expense to honor a marriage that would never be.

She had another worry. Not once had Wilburn contacted her. Not once. On the Saturday before the Fourth of July, she finished off the week's baking and loaded the dishwasher with cookie sheets while wondering—for the thousandth time—where he was and what he was doing. Had he done anything with the machinery blueprints? Had he made any strides with Texas Bakeries? Was he all right?

Of course Cade continued to be elusive. Even more so after their evening ride. She got the impression he was avoiding her. Why?

"You don't have much to say today," Cade's housekeeper commented in her heavily accented English. "Are you unwell?"

"Oh, no, I'm fine," Maureen assured and smiled at Frieda Wittig. "Just a little preoccupied, that's all."

"Thinking about Mr. Cade?"

"Of course not."

"There is no need to be shy, *Mädchen*. I know he isn't the easiest man to love."

Maureen, her fingers twitching, measured dishwasher detergent into the well. "Love him? Sometimes I don't even like him."

Now why did she say that? Especially in front of his employee! Maureen could have bitten her tongue.

"We all feel that way about men at times, *Mädchen*. One moment, we want to strangle our men, the next . . . we want nothing more than to hold them in our arms."

"Well said." She grinned at Frieda. The housekeeper was a kindly person and had shown valor in allowing Maureen to share her domain. Frieda was a marvel. Although Maureen had been antsy to ask her about a lot of subjects, to this point she hadn't. She hadn't felt comfortable, thinking about such talk with Cade's employee. But since Cade had refused to discuss so many things about himself, Maureen had to find out just what made him tick. She eased into the subject now with Frieda. "How long have you worked for Cade?"

"For seven years. I was nurse to his *Mutter*—his mother—during her last sickness. For two years, I took care of her." Frieda wiped her hands on a dishtowel. "She was a *gnädige Frau*. A gracious lady, always kind and sweet to me . . . and to everyone else."

"She was?" She had always assumed that Rowena was nastiness personified. Maureen poured two cups of coffee, and knowing Frieda enjoyed a snifter of schnapps in her evening coffee, she went for the liquor cabinet. She poured the housekeeper a shot into her cup, then, living dangerously, gave herself an equal amount. "Did you know that Cade and I are related?" Maureen asked, taking her cup to her lips.

"*Ja.*"

"Do you know why he resents his dad?"

"I do not."

The housekeeper polished off her drink, and Maureen fixed her another one. "Frieda, the first day I met you, I got the impression you were glad to see me. Why?"

"It is not good, a son hating his father. When I opened the door, I felt something right here in my heart." She patted her breastbone. "I sensed you are a good girl and a peacemaker. And I prayed you would heal Mr. Cade's heart." She chuckled. "I did not know you would work miracles this soon." A dreamy look in her eyes, she said, "Imagine . . . a wedding."

Maureen shifted uncomfortably. Only once had Cade made real plans for marriage. "What happened between him and Pamela Patton?"

"It is not for me to tell."

"I know you're loyal to Cade, but I'm trying to understand him."

Frieda, her gray eyebrows knitted, stared at her cup, then ran her thumb across its rim. Finished, she pulled a cigarette from her apron and lit the cylindrical tip. Past a curled ribbon of smoke, she riveted her eyes to Maureen's. "Miss

Pam was a fortune hunter. She married *der Riese* Jake Patton for *Geld*. Mr. Cade was a penniless college student.''

"But the Pemberton family always had money. I've always known that."

"You are mistaken, Miss Maureen. Frau Herrington had no money. Her company had been bankrupt for many years when I was employed. Mr. Cade got into college with a scholarship, and he worked after school for spending money."

Taken aback, Maureen couldn't believe her ears. Always, she had assumed that Cade had inherited money from his mother's side of the family. Wilburn had said as much. Had he lied? She delved into the recesses of her brain, searching for answers, and realized he had said that Rowena had inherited Pemberton Couplings. Nothing more. Maureen's assumptions had been grand. She had figured wealth followed forever. How wrong she had been, and her admiration for Cade grew to huge proportions. He had not only started from nothing, he had achieved everything. Everything but love. And love was life's most important and fulfilling asset.

She wanted to show him love.

Chapter Seven

How can a woman show a man love when he stays away from her? Cade took leave of the Dry Hole and didn't reappear. But Maureen had her rationalizations. Only a few days had passed, and word reached her that he was out of town on business. But she would have her chance tonight at the dinner party in his Fortuna penthouse.

July the Fourth had dawned clear as crystal and dry as cotton. A card arrived in the mail that morning. Wilburn sent his love and best wishes. There was no return address, and the postmark was smeared. Maureen would have preferred his presence, especially on this, her twenty-fourth birthday.

Beyond the anniversary of her birth, Independence Day meant many things to Maureen. Hot dogs, watermelon, snow cones, cotton candy. Sparklers and as many Roman candles as the pocketbook allowed. Picnics in the park, complete with ants. No picnic was a true picnic without insects! But there would be no ants today.

A trip to the beauty shop left her face glowing from a facial, her hair shining and upswept, and her fingernails in top-notch condition. They were still short, but nail polish did wonders.

She dressed with care for the dinner. Her high heels matched the strapless white evening gown that showed off her beginning tan—she'd made use of Cade's swimming pool during a few free hours. Her accessories were the pearl ear studs and two-strand choker that Wilburn had given her mother as an anniversary gift—a present that took him three years to pay for. Maureen wasn't a woman to gawk at herself in the mirror, but tonight she approved of her appearance. The question in her mind was, would Cade find her attractive?

In his downtown penthouse, as they awaited the guests' arrival, Maureen noticed Cade's appearance, and not for the first time that evening. He wore a black tuxedo, not an ornate one, and see-yourself-in-the-shine black shoes. His dark hair was slicked back in a *GQ* style, and no New York wheeler-dealer ever looked better. His presence dominated the great room.

"Did I miss a spot, shaving?" he teased while handing her a glass of white wine. "You've been staring at me all evening."

Abashed at being caught, she decided to ignore his question. Although she had vowed to show him love, the doing was harder than the promising. She was new at this game, and she felt her naïveté creep up.

She turned from the room that held the look of a slick magazine layout but none of the comfortable, undecorated air of the ranch, and opened the balcony's sliding glass doors to stare at the San Antonio skyline. This wasn't a city of skyscrapers. The summer sun, waning but still bright, lit the River Walk's crowded promenade and the river barges loaded with revelers. Already, crowds had gathered around the Alamo and Hemisfair Plaza areas. A band was playing, its amplified sounds distorted at Maureen's seventh-floor perch. People were dancing to the music and awaiting the midnight fireworks display. San Antonian's took their partying seriously. Three annual events brought them out in droves. New Year's Eve, Fiesta in April, and the Fourth of July.

What was the matter with her, thinking about festivities when the most attractive man she had ever met in her life was standing on the other side of the sliding door? Yes, he was forceful, but that appealed to Maureen. She wasn't the shrinking-violet type, for crying out loud! Never had the puppy-dog-at-heel type of man appealed to her. She wanted to be challenged.

As if on cue, Cade stepped onto the balcony, and Maureen whirled around. "Did I say something offensive?" he asked, closing the door.

"No, but I must admit, it startled me, getting caught. Yes, I was staring at you. You're a good-looking man, Cade Herrington. I'd be blind not to look at you."

"Same goes here. You're a knockout, Maureen. That dark hair of yours, those blue eyes. They... Well, that dress sets your coloring off to perfection. Every man who's seen you tells me what a lucky guy I am."

He took her hand, leading her to the balcony's sofa, and Maureen warmed to her man.

Drawing her to his lap, he said, "I'm proud of you. You've done a great job being my fiancée."

There he went again, turning the conversation to business, but she refused to be put off by his statement. Expensive after-shave tickled her senses while warmth above the July temperature beat through her veins. The tip of her forefinger traced his ear; she felt his muscles quiver. Pleased that she could affect him, she scanned each of his features in turn. "Must we always talk about business, Cade? Can't we simply leave it at—I like your looks and you like mine?" She moistened her lips and decided boldness was going to be her new byword. "Shall we seal it with a kiss?"

Caught off guard, Cade rounded his eyes; his muscles were taut as a fiddle string. A growl rolled from his throat as the fingers of one hand brushed her collarbone. She repeated her question, but he cleared his throat and collected himself. Somehow he managed to move Maureen off his lap. Planted at the sofa's end, he crossed his legs. Why was he being ornery? she wondered.

"I, uh, we do have a little more business to settle before the guests arrive." He dug into a pocket. "You'd better wear this."

A ring winked in the early-evening sunlight. "This ... that's an engagement ring! Cade, surely you didn't buy an expensive ring for ... I can't wear it."

Her declaration ignored, he took her hand and slipped the piece of jewelry on the proper finger. "Diamonds for tradition, sapphires for your eyes. It's fitting."

Fitting? An engagement ring should have had a promise of the future. This one might have weighed a hundred pounds. It was beautiful, though, and her feminine emotions ran rampant. Was it wrong to pretend—only for a moment—that it was a true engagement ring?

"Don't look like that," he ordered softly. "It's not the end of the world. It's just a ring."

"Maybe to you ... but, Cade, I'm not worldly like you are. You've accused me of being sentimental, and I am. I've dreamed of having a ring on my finger, but I don't want it to be for a charade." She looked away. "I'm sorry, but I don't feel right wearing the ring."

He slid his arm around her shoulder. "I'm sorry, too, honey. I guess I wasn't thinking." Leaning toward her and pulling her close, he placed a soft kiss on her forehead. "It's just that . . . well, you lead me such a merry chase at times. I forget how young you are."

"Twenty-four isn't *that* young."

"Twenty-four? You're that old," he replied jokingly. "Good Lord, woman, you'll be coloring the gray and wearing foot-saver shoes in no time."

She had to force herself to match his light tone. "Watch it now. You'll always be my senior, Mr. Herrington. Eleven years ahead of my gray hair and bunions."

"Neither one of us is getting any younger. We ought to think about settling down while we can still attract the opposite sex." He caressed her smooth shoulder. "Have you ever thought about it, settling down?"

Surely Maureen had heard wrong. Cade the confirmed bachelor discussing forever after? Had she had too much to drink? Was she caught in some wonderful fantasy? Yet he had said those words, and she vowed not to make too much of them. Surely he had been speaking . . . hypothetically.

"Yes, I've thought of settling down. I'm not a confirmed bachelorette. I want a man to call my own. And children."

"How many children?"

"Scads of them."

His mouth opened a fraction, just a tiny bit, and he swallowed. "The father of this brood . . . Tell me, sweetheart, what would be his qualifications?"

"Qualifications?"

"What would you look for in a man."

It was Maureen's turn to break the embrace. She needed a bit of space, since telling Cade that he was the man for her would be rushing things. "Actually, I've been too busy over the years to think about it."

Was that disappointment in his expressive features? But he was quick on recovering, she noted.

"I'd like to hear more about those busy years," he said.

"You know I've had a time with the cookie factory. It's taken all my energies for three years. Before that, well, I had my hands full taking care of Mama."

"Wilburn didn't help?"

"Oh, yes. But Mama was sick for a long time, and it took both of our efforts to care for her."

Cade frowned. "He was pretty good about it—helping out?"

"The best. He was devoted to her."

The expression Maureen had come to know well, a hardening of facial muscles, set Cade's countenance. "My mother wasn't so fortunate. He never did her anything but wrong."

Delight that he was confiding in her warred with Maureen's disbelief and concern over his statement. But at long last, he was talking, and it pleased her that he was ready to share his secrets.

"I've hated him for a long time, Maureen. Almost forever. And I'll never forgive him for what he did to my mother." He squeezed his eyes. "She was the perfect wife and mother, but he never appreciated her. He cheated on her, Maureen. And he didn't try to deny it. When she asked for a divorce, Wilburn wanted more. He wanted cash. He left us, and his fists were clutching Pemberton money."

She refused to believe Cade's statement, but Maureen wanted to comfort him. "I'm sorry, Cade. So sorry."

"Don't be sorry, honey. Learn from the lesson."

She wouldn't argue, albeit believing his words was impossible as the sun setting in the east. Wilburn Herrington wasn't the philandering type, and as for his taking Pemberton money—hogwash! After his divorce, he had been destitute.

"You don't believe me, do you?" Cade asked.

"I believe you believe it. And I'd like to know *why* you do. Maybe your mother—" she was grasping at straws, since Frieda had said Rowena was a *gnädige Frau* "—maybe she wanted you to think the worst about—"

"You leave my mother out of this."

His quick defense spoke for itself. "I'm right, aren't I?" Maureen asked and regretted it when Cade lunged to his feet, hurt ravaging his expression. She had touched an open wound. "Oh, Cade, forgive me. I'm sorry for what I said, sorry for you. And for your dad, because he isn't a scoundrel."

Cade went to the railing and studied the festival crowd before doing an about-face. His eyes were hard, cold, bitter. "From the day you showed up at my office, you've been nagging me about my problem with Wilburn. Now you know how I feel. Don't *ever* mention the subject again."

Maureen would have gladly stitched her mouth closed. Why in the name of heck hadn't she simply let Cade do the talking? How had she ever imagined that showing him love would include disagreeing with him? *You're the argumentative type, that's why.* Especially when it came to Wilburn's integrity.

"Let's go back in," Cade said. "The guests will be here any minute." His shoulders stiff, he marched away from the balcony.

And the ring was still on her finger.

At a quarter after eight, Douglas Smythe made an appearance. Alone. Sandra, he said proudly, would be arriving with her husband. Maureen was in no frame of mind to bubble over the good news, not with friction arcing between herself and Cade.

His conduct switched from anger to obvious pleasure upon hearing about the Uhrs, though, and he began to behave as if he and Maureen hadn't exchanged words on the balcony. She knew he was still troubled. He felt strongly about *everything*. She had witnessed his temper, his thinly veiled hurt, his occasional offhandedness. As for the nonchalance, she surmised that it was nothing more than a defense mechanism.

Covertly, she eyed the object of her concern. He was instructing the uniformed caterers, his words and movements pure confidence and power. He had a lot going for him. Beyond his physical attractiveness, he was shrewd and crafty, dedicated to business and successful at it, but he was much more than a money-making machine. He was compassionate toward those around him. Of course, there was an exception... Wilburn.

Poor Wilburn. It seemed impossible, fighting a dead woman's damning word. And that had to be the problem's root. Rowena must have poisoned Cade's mind. Poor Cade.

The intercom buzzed, cutting off Maureen's intent study.

"Mr. and Mrs. Jake Patton to see you," announced the squawky guard from his post in the Fortuna Building's lobby.

A couple of minutes later, the polished bronze elevator doors slid open to allow the couple entrance. Jake was boorish as ever. His cigar ashes never hit an ashtray, his huge feet were parked on the chinoiserie coffee table. Talking nonstop, his subjects centered on himself or his "ain't-she-wonderful" wife. Maureen could hardly abide either Patton—Jake on general principles, Pam for hurting Cade all those years ago.

Again the guard alerted them to visitors. Sandra, wearing chiffon and a radiant smile, clutched her husband's arm. Phil Uhr wore a tuxedo cut in the same style as his host's, though Cade looked much better in his. Behind the horn-rimmed glasses perched on his thin nose, Phil's eyes never left his wife.

As hostess, Maureen led the guests to the table. The caterer's staff ebbed and flowed as smoothly as the fine wine went down her throat. Everything was elegant and beautifully appointed. Tropical flowers centered the huge oval table, and two candelabra with genuine beeswax candles cast a soft glow over the wainscoted dining room. Jake doused his cigar in a finger bowl.

Neither she nor Cade ate much of the dinner.

By the dessert course, she had felt Phil Uhr's shoeless foot at her ankle three times; Maureen's leg had gotten in the way of his journey to Sandra's foot. Apparently the Uhrs were well on their way to reconciliation.

Douglas Smythe pushed back his chair and got to his feet. "I'd like to propose a toast to the happy couple." He lifted his glass. "Here's to Maureen and Cade. May their marriage be filled with love and their home with children."

Maureen blushed. Jake Patton spilled champagne on the Irish-linen tablecloth. Sandra looked at Phil, who was mooning like a puppy at his wife. Pamela swallowed a bite of Bananas Foster, then lifted her glass.

Cade accepted the toast. "Thank you, Doug."

The party retired to the great room. The Pattons and Douglas sat in chairs while Cade guided Maureen to the huge sectional sofa. Phil and Sandra took a temporary leave to make use of the balcony for "a breath of air." Cade and Douglas grinned in satisfaction.

Lighting yet another cigar, Jake leaned the wing chair back on two legs. The joints protested. "Y'all set a date yet?"

A date? Of course not. Maureen fidgeted, trying to come up with a plausible sounding reply.

"Don't tell me it's not set in concrete," Jake said, sneering. "Why, I'd think you weren't serious."

"We have thought about it," Cade replied and put his arm around Maureen's shoulders. "We're going to be married on October first. The tenth anniversary of my first gusher."

"That'll be after the elections, won't it?" Jake's mean little eyes were on Cade. "I'd say that's right convenient."

"How so?" Maureen asked.

Cade squeezed her hand and did the answering. "Of course it's convenient, Jake. We don't want the elections cutting into our honeymoon time, do we, sweetheart?"

With the tenor of a Mack truck's engine, the gargantuan Jake Patton piped up. "You're hoping to win the presidency and then you're planning to neglect your duties—if you ever have those duties—to take a honeymoon. Doesn't sound like you, Herrington. Not at all."

Pamela patted her dark chignon, then pursed her generous lips. "Jake, darling, what's the matter with you? Where's your sense of romance? Leave them alone."

Douglas muttered a "Hear, hear" in accordance with Pamela's advice. A waiter offered cognac, and Maureen was relieved at the interruption.

"Tell me, Maureen, have you chosen a church?" Pamela asked.

Jake Patton rolled his smoke to the opposite side of his mouth and gave rapt attention to the forthcoming answer.

Good gravy, another question without an answer. Bits of remembrances tumbled in her mind, recollections of her mother's marriage to Wilburn. "We've decided on Nuevo Laredo."

Cade nearly choked on his cognac.

What a dumb thing to say. People like Cade don't make a run for the Mexican border to get married. But she was in it this far, and Maureen had to continue. "We don't want a big to-do. I'd feel awful, taking Cade away from his work. Something simple appeals to both of us. Doesn't it, darling?"

Cade set his drink aside. "Right." He imparted an unreadable look his "bride's" way.

"For heaven's sake," Douglas protested, "you can't be serious. That's socially unacceptable. Everyone will be expecting to attend the nuptials. And surely you'll want a religious service, once you've given it more thought."

"We have given it thought, Doug," Cade said, brooking no argument.

Pamela placed her glass down. "Jake and I can't stay. Mother's watching the kids, and she likes to turn in early."

There is a God. The Pattons are leaving.

The couple said their farewells, and the Uhrs returned to the great room.

A proud smile on his thin features, Phil Uhr squeezed his wife's shoulder. "Sandra and I have an announcement. We're getting back together."

Douglas grabbed his daughter in a bear hug, then slapped his son-in-law's back. Cade moved to shake Phil's hand and kiss Sandra's cheek. The repercussions of Cade achieving his goal didn't sink in to Maureen, and she joined the happy crowd. All her romanticist's heart knew at this moment was that Sandra was back with the man she loved. Who wouldn't be pleased?

The guests as well as the staff had departed. Maureen had a problem, now that realization had dawned. The Uhrs were back together, so where did that leave her plans to reconcile father and son? Where did that leave the mock engagement? With no reason for Cade to continue with the pretense, would he dismiss her from his life?

Shucking his tux jacket, Cade loosened his tie and the top three buttons of his dress shirt. The dark chest hair above the V caused Maureen to smile, regardless of her anxieties. Sexy was the only way to describe him.

"Congratulations, Cade," she murmured, drinking in the long form of the man she loved. "You got what you wanted."

His voice was a husky whisper as he took a step toward her. "Not everything I want."

Figuring his statement had something to do with their argument, she said, "I'd like to apologize about...about earlier this evening."

"Forget it. I'm not in the mood for apologies or rehashing yesterdays, and I hope you aren't, either."

"But I—"

"I will say this," he cut in. "I was proud of you tonight. As usual, you were perfect. Except for the Nuevo Laredo thing." He chuckled. "I could've throttled you over that."

"I can be impossible at times."

"That's part of your charm, kiddo. I never know what to expect out of you." He winked. "You're a real firecracker."

She didn't know whether to be pleased or insulted, and before she could settle her mind, Cade threw his arms wide and said, "I feel like celebrating!"

"As well you should. Sandra and Phil—"

"Forget them. I'm wanting to celebrate—" Cade leaned down to pull a package from its hiding place behind the sofa. Offering it to Maureen, he whispered, "Happy birthday."

Her hand shook as she grasped the box. "B-but how did you know...?"

"Silly girl, have you forgotten I make it my business to know everything that concerns me?" he asked lightly.

Maureen recalled his investigation of Granny Miniver's Famous. In the past it had been a sore subject, but now his snooping wasn't a bother. Shrewdness was part of his appeal. And she was pleased he had investigated her birthday—more pleased at his remembrance than over the gift. And when she unwrapped the package, she wasn't quite so certain about that.

"Oh, Cade, it's— It's wonderful!" Her fingers gripped the handle of a large silver spoon. "But it's too nice to use for cookies."

"Granted, it's mostly ornamental. Turn it over, Maureen, and read the inscription."

She did.

"To the world's sweetest cookie. Keep up the good work. I'm proud of you. Love, Cade"

Love, Cade? If only that were true....

It was simply a nicety such as a letter's closing. But he hadn't been forced to have anything inscribed, she reminded herself. Whether his feelings were love or cordiality or whatever, this gift was personal, not business, and although it was no dime-store trinket, the spoon represented a giving of self rather than of money.

Darned if she didn't feel a tear roll down her cheek.

"Hey," he said, drawing out the word, "don't cry." He took the spoon from her hand and set it aside. "It's only an attagirl."

"Maybe so, but it's the most wonderful back pat I've ever gotten."

Turning off the waterworks was impossible. She loved this man . . . he was wonderful . . . and probably unattainable. When he pulled her to his broad chest, his fingers spreading across the exposed skin of her back, she wilted against him. "Gads," she said a few moments later, "I'm messing up your shirt."

"That's a small price to pay for . . ." His finger moved to dry her cheekbone. "You know, the night's still young." He glanced at the clock. "A quarter of twelve. How would you like to spend the rest of your birthday?"

Cuddled against that broad chest would be a nice start. "You'll think I'm crazy," she said.

"Try me."

"I was thinking along the line of firecrackers."

"Hmm. Firecrackers. I think something can be arranged." A smile crinkling the corners of his eyes, he linked his arm with hers. "We've got the best seat in town. Come this way." On the balcony, he pointed to the Tower of the Americas. "Best place in town to watch the attractions," he said meaningfully, his gaze on Maureen.

Goose bumps rose on her arms. She was very near moving into his arms. She wanted to be there. While she ached to make a real relationship out of their sham, Maureen was wise enough to know they were moving too fast. Cade was experienced with women, while her experience with the opposite sex had been limited to a few kisses, and it would be unwise—if not downright dangerous!—to get involved in a sexual relationship.

And that's all it would be on Cade's part. Sex. When she gave herself in the true sense of the word, Maureen wanted it to be right and forever. She wanted it to be that way with

Cade, but . . . This could be their final time together, what with the Uhrs reconciled.

"W-we have a marvelous view," she said, "but we're missing half the fun."

"I wouldn't agree."

She grabbed his big, square hand. "Cade Herrington, where's your sense of adventure? You and I are going to the party!"

Within five minutes they were on the grounds in front of the Alamo, bastion of Texas independence. Laughing, dancing, singing along with the music from the bandstand, a throng of people surrounded the complex. A kaleidoscope of colors brightened the night, and the sounds of exploding fireworks filled Maureen's ears. A whiff of acrid smoke tickled her nose, but it didn't bother her; it was part of the celebration. Spying the food stands, and inhaling their tempting aromas, she could barely resist the sizzling hot dogs, the cotton candy, the candied apples. Maureen was starving. But after that elegant dinner, would she be an ingrate to suggest . . . ?

She would. "Let's walk over to La Villita," she suggested. Hopefully, there wouldn't be any food over there.

With Cade in the lead, they wound their way to the restored old town opposite Hemisfair Plaza. The area wasn't as densely populated as the old mission grounds. But, drat, wasn't that a pretzel stand?

Cade pointed up at the sky. "Wonder what they call those thingumabobs."

She sat down on a low retaining wall. "Catherine wheel firecrackers, that's what. Don't you know anything?" she ribbed, patting the seat next to her.

He sat down. "Never had much chance to mull their names. I've always been a great admirer of fireworks, though. They light the night, charge your life."

This very evening Cade had called her a firecracker. Then, she hadn't known how to take his remark, but now she was quite honored.

"Since you like exploding lights, I'm amazed you didn't take time to find out more about them." He didn't respond, and she pressed, "I thought all kids... You didn't buy them when you were a child?"

"Sparklers, that's about it. By the time I was old enough for the better stuff, Wilburn was...out of the picture."

Naturally Maureen wanted to press the subject with the zeal of a courthouse reporter, but Cade had warned her not to mention his father again, and she wouldn't. She wanted to enjoy their night together...what could be their last night together.

"Know what, Maureen... I'm famished," Cade admitted. "Think I could interest you in a beer and a hot dog?"

"Only if you include cotton candy."

Hugging an arm around her waist, he replied, "Woman, you drive a hard bargain."

It was 3:00 a.m. before the taxi deposited them at the Dry Hole Ranch. After an evening of reveling, Cade had refused—to Maureen's swift agreement—to get behind the wheel.

Before he went to his bedroom, he gave her a good-night kiss. With the time period of their business arrangement unsettled, she pulled away before the embrace heated up.

In the privacy of her suite of rooms, she placed her precious spoon on the bedside table, then headed for the bathroom. Her next stop was the medicine cabinet for an antacid. Too much food and drink had taken its toll. Or was her roiling tummy caused by emotional distress, now that she was left alone to ponder the future?

She chewed the chalky tablets and turned to the mirror. It told a gruesome tale. Pieces of pink cotton candy were stuck in her hair and on her cheek. Her beautiful new evening gown had a purple stain on the bodice, the drippings of a snow cone. She recalled that Cade's shirt had a big dollop of mustard on the sleeve. He hadn't seemed to mind. In fact, when he had dropped the mustard-coated pretzel, he laughed and kissed her nose.

Fifi sidled into the bathroom to twist her lithe body around Maureen's ankle, and she drew the cat into her arms to nuzzle the marmalade fur. Over a series of purrs, Maureen said, "Hiya, kitty cat. You and I have gotten to be good friends, haven't we? We haven't told Cade about that huge box of gourmet cat goodies I have hidden in the bedside table. That's our secret."

Charming as a debutante, Fifi lowered her eyelids in concordance.

Maureen kicked off her high heels, walked to bed and sank onto the bedspread, the feline with her. Her fingers delved into the hiding place and she extracted a much-appreciated treat. Fifi begged for another, but her efforts were in vain.

"You know, Feef, being with Cade was fun beyond my wildest imagination. Sandra's name never came up in conversation. We were just a man and a woman enjoying the Fourth of July. And each other. It was my best birthday."

The cat cuddled against her.

"Do you think there's a chance that your master might be . . . might be interested in more than a business deal? Oh, Fifi, sweetie, wouldn't that be wonderful!" Maureen paused. "I'm being a romantic fool. Okay, he's told me he'd like to have sex, and he was carefree on the streets of San Antonio, but he's never said *anything* to encourage me about the future. Dratted man. What am I going to do about him? Do about him? Huh. The question is—what's he going to do about me? Sandra's back with her husband, so I serve Cade no purpose.''

Had she jumped to a conclusion?

Maureen picked up the silver spoon and clutched it to her bosom. Cade hadn't said anything to indicate long-term interest, but there was tangible evidence that he felt something for her.

Or was she being silly, jumping to the conclusion that he might care for her? Yes, the latter part of this night had been marvelous, but what would dawn bring?

Chapter Eight

Dawn brought a headache. Unaccustomed as she was to late hours, Maureen's forehead pounded. The makings of forty dozen cookies awaited in the ranch kitchen—for the first time, not a pleasing proposition. The biggest part of the *mal de tête?* Being in limbo with Cade. What with last night, she wanted to believe he was interested in more than business—monkey or otherwise. Yet she wouldn't allow the luxury of optimism. Their time together, on the whole, didn't add up to hope.

As she worked alongside Janece Stewart, baking cookies and preparing them for delivery, Maureen feared Cade would stride into the kitchen and tell her goodbye. By ten he still hadn't made an appearance for his usual breakfast of cookies and coffee. Each passing moment doubled her apprehension. It wasn't like him to sleep in, Maureen fretted. Was he rehearsing the farewell speech?

"I feel lousy," she announced to her assistant and retrieved a bottle of aspirin. "Think I'll take a break."

Janece was the epitome of concern. "Sit down, gal. You're not gonna be sick, are you?" Receiving a head shake in reply, the redhead fetched a glass of water. "Drink this. Nice and slow. That's a girl." She took a chair close to Maureen. "Feeling better?"

"A little, thank you," Maureen replied honestly.

"Good thing we're on half schedule today. I don't think you could make it through a whole day."

"I tend to agree."

Janece poured her boss a cup of coffee, then added sugar and cream. As Maureen sipped the sweetened brew, the older woman said, "I can finish up. Why don't you make use of the sun and that fantastic swimming pool of Cade's? Betcha anything it'll make you feel one-hundred-percent."

"I doubt it."

Peering over her half glasses, Janece asked, "What's the matter?"

"Lack of sleep."

"Then a snooze on a chaise longue should come in mighty handy."

"Sleep won't help me." Maureen shucked her disposable gloves and hair net, then tightened her ponytail. "I've got... It's just that ... I'm worried about me and Cade." She proceeded to fill Janece in on the situation and finished with "I don't want to lose him."

"Have you told him? You know, that you care for him?"

"Not in so many words. But I have made a few remarks."

"Subtly, I'm sure," Janece came back dryly.

Maureen laughed at herself. "You know I'm not subtle."

Apparently this was a comment needing no further discussion. Janece got up to fill a stack of boxes with Granny Miniver's Famous. During those motions—work done without a murmur passing between the two women—Maureen was lost in dread. Where was Cade, who by his absence was making the morning so tense? He wasn't the sissy type, he faced most problems head-on, so why didn't he simply walk into the kitchen and tell her to pack her bags?

"Heard anything from Wilburn?"

Janece's question yanked Maureen out of her brown study. "A birthday card. Yesterday."

"Did he mention how he's doing with Cade's money and idea? Did he say anything about Texas Bakeries?"

Discussing Wilburn Herrington was never a good subject with Janece. But that didn't stop Maureen's thoughts. Regarding the rift between the two Herrington men, he was as closemouthed and exasperating as Cade. But as soon as Maureen got a moment alone with the elder one, she *would* get him to talk.

That moment, nonetheless, might come too late for her to do anything more with her peacemaking.

"Well, Maureen, what about Wilburn?"

Maureen didn't wish to get into it. "The fireworks were wonderful last night. You should have seen them."

"Mother and I saw them. We parked in the King William district. The view was fine. But you didn't answer my question." Scrunching her mouth into a moue of aggravation, she stapled her gaze to Maureen. "I'd say the esteemed Mr. Wilburn Herrington didn't say one word about money or ideas or his progress in Dallas. I doubt you'll hear from him again."

"Jan, you have no call to say that."

"None but concern," Janece answered. "I may be your employee, but I've always considered myself your friend, a friend who's lent an ear on more than one occasion. I worry about you. It hurts me to see you troubled over your stepfather. I think you should forget he's alive—he's as much as done that with you. Concentrate on Cade. He's the one you love, the one who can return that love.''

"You're jumping to conclusions.''

"I don't think so. Maureen, honey, I've watched the way that man looks at you. He's hungry-eyed. I'd be willing to bet my week's salary he's wanting you as much as you want him.''

"If that were true, I wouldn't be standing in this kitchen, pouring my heart out to you.''

"Phooey. I've seen a lot in my thirty-five years, and I can assure you that love plays wicked little games. You're one of the most straightforward women I've ever met, but you hesitate to come right out and say 'Cade, I love you, so let's forget the business deal.' I imagine he's suffering under the same uncertainties.'' Her emerald-green eyes were soft, and Janece reached to squeeze Maureen's hand. "Very rarely are relationships cut-and-dried. Don't give up on yours.''

"*I* haven't done that. Second-guessing Cade's frame of mind is another matter, Jan, because you may have seen something in him that isn't there.'' She got up from the chair. "I'll give you one thing, though. That swimming pool idea is beginning to sound better and better.''

Within ten minutes she was wearing her swimsuit, a blue two-piece that Cade had selected during their shopping trip. She grabbed a towel and slid her feet into sandals—and all the while she couldn't stop thinking about Janece's words. Was it possible that Cade loved her?

Even if he did, a little someone came between them. His father. Wilburn was her father, too; not in blood but in heart. Although she loved her mother's widower with all the daughterly affection in the world, the fact remained: he had been lax in keeping in touch.

Plus, she recalled Cade's charges about infidelity. Could it be true? He had lost visitation rights to his son. Which had to indicate some sort of guilt along some sort of line. Something—several things—didn't add up about Wilburn's past, so maybe he *had* treated his first family shabbily. Maureen could no longer automatically defend him.

If only she could get him alone. . . .

Given her strong feelings for his son, she couldn't spend the rest of her life wondering what went wrong between the two men she loved. She was just too curious for that. That was how she tried to rationalize it all. A curious nature. Phooey, as Jan would say.

She glanced at her bed, where the queenly Fifi was reposing. The cat yawned and stretched, her fetching eyes staring back at Maureen.

Temporarily diverted from her anxieties, Maureen asked, "How about a treat?"

Fifi stretched a foreleg, unsheathed her claws and glided over to the bedside table.

The kibble given to its ardent admirer, Maureen dropped the box in the table drawer. "Like Janece suggested, I'm going to make use of the sun. Maybe it'll dry my soggy brain."

Maureen made her way downstairs, outside and down the staircase to the free-form pool situated on the terrace at ground level above the deck. She halted at the bottom of the steps, her heart thumping against her chest. No more than twenty feet from her vantage point, she stared at the craggy countryside . . . and Cade.

Sunlight and water glistened in his raven-black hair, and on the fit lines of his tall, lean frame. Wearing white swim briefs that hugged his narrow hips and set off his tan to bronzed perfection, he stood on the springboard, his arms lifted skyward. Maureen blew a stream of breath past her pursed lips as he dove into the pool. Fluid as a fish, he swam the pool's length before surfacing. Seconds later, he levered to the pool deck and got to his feet, his hand running across the dark mat of his broad chest. Even Hercules didn't have a better physique, she thought and smiled.

But her smile faded when Cade caught sight of her. He started to return her expression—she knew he did—but turned away and grabbed a towel to dry his face. Not a good sign.

Going with Janece's advice to admit her love? It seemed as wise as running naked through San Antonio's barrios. Hesitantly, Maureen walked over to him.

"Morning," she said, voice trembling. "Mind if I join you?"

He turned away and busied himself toweling his body. "Actually, I've done my laps. Need to get to the office. But help yourself. Water's fine."

"Why don't you want to talk to me?" she asked and dreaded his answer.

She watched him swallow. And his eyes took a brief glance at her body...before yanking away to a point beyond her shoulder.

"If you want the truth..." The firm line of his mouth tugged into a half frown. "I can't put it in words."

The craziest feeling grabbed Maureen. She warmed to his uncertainty—it was so unlike Cade and she found him even more appealing...if possible. Yet she couldn't disregard the fact he was uncomfortable in her presence.

"Shall I give it a try?" she asked.

"I won't have you putting words in my mouth." He took an about-face, going for a chair. "And we might as well—" He halted and crossed his arms. "Uh oh. Here comes Sandra."

Drat. Darn. Blast it! The last thing Maureen wanted at that moment was a visit from Mrs. Phil Uhr.

Sandra bore a wedding gift, elegantly wrapped and about the size of a shirt box.

"I hope you don't mind the intrusion." She placed the package on the umbrella table and took a chair next to it. "But I wanted to bring this by, and I figured there was no time like the present."

No time like the present? Maureen chuckled inwardly, nervously, at that age-old phrase. There couldn't be a worse time as far as she was concerned, what with so much to be settled with Cade, but she said nary a word of protest.

Instead, she wilted onto a chair across from Sandra, sensing rather than seeing Cade seat himself next to her. She could smell the slightly chlorinated water that adhered to his muscled form; the heat of him radiated to envelop her arm, her thigh. Normally being this close to him had a marked and luscious effect on Maureen. Right now, she was a wreck.

"Your ring is lovely," Sandra said. "I meant to comment on it last night."

It was all Maureen could do not to cover her hand. After her it-doesn't-feel-right-to-wear-it speech to Cade, she hadn't taken it off. And evidently he noticed the same. He arched a brow at her blushing face.

"I've been trying to figure out why you guys are in a rush for Nuevo Laredo," Sandra commented. "Cade, you hate tawdry border towns."

"I, uh, we're not going for the local color. You know how it is, Sandra, you've been a newlywed. Need I remind you we won't see much of the town?" He laced his fingers with his temporary fiancée's and artfully changed the topic. "Speaking of days spent in honeymooning heaven, where will you and Phil be taking your second one?"

"I...we haven't discussed it. We're under the same roof, but we still have a few problems to work out."

Maureen felt Cade tense.

Sandra heaved a sigh. "Listen, I'm not here to discuss me and Phil." Picking up the package, she held it toward Maureen. "Go on, open it. I can't wait!" Her countenance was as bright as a child's. "Go on!"

With no gracious way of declining, Maureen undid the wrappings. The interior held a wealth of tissue paper, and beneath...a vellum envelope. Maureen handed it to Cade. "You do the honors...darling."

He did. "Two weeks at Klosters."

"Where's that?" Maureen asked.

"In Switzerland, sweetheart."

"The trip starts October second," Sandra explained. "That'll give you a day in transit from Mexico to Europe. I know it's off-season, but the Alps are lovely, any time of year." A genuine smile to her delicate features, she winked. "If you two are determined to elope, at least do your honeymoon in style."

"Sounds good to me." His teeth flashing, Cade smiled at Maureen. "How does it sound to you, sweetheart?"

"I—I don't know."

Sandra waved her manicured fingernails. "Humor me. I'm accustomed to getting my way, and I want you to have the trip."

Being handed a dream honeymoon was more than Maureen could bear. She recalled how hurt Sandra had been on the day of the barbecue, how Cade had manipulated the whole thing and how she had gone along with him. This offering had peace written all over it. Sandra deserved better than she had gotten. *Why doesn't the earth open up and swallow me?*

"You're awfully nice to offer," Maureen said, her throat scratchy, "but we can't accept such a gift."

She felt the side of Cade's foot thumping her ankle.

Evidently Sandra caught Maureen's chagrin. "I understand why you want to keep your distance from me," she said. "That day at the lake...well, that was hurt talking. Even then, I didn't want to make an enemy of you. Do you...Can you forgive me?"

"That goes without saying." But how would Sandra feel if she discovered that she had been plotted against?

"You know, Maureen, Cade and I have been...pals for a long time. And I'd like to be friends with you, too. Do you think that's possible?"

Never had animosity toward Sandra been part of her feelings. In fact, Maureen rather liked her and always had. They had nothing in common, but... "I'd very much like to be your friend, Sandra. Very much."

"Then don't reject my wedding gift." The blonde reached to hug Maureen. "And I'm leaving before you can say another word." Which she did.

Alone with Cade and her guilty conscience, Maureen felt lower than a worm. A shiver racked her bones, despite the Texas heat. Hugging her arms, she walked to the pool's edge and stared with unseeing eyes at its blue depths. Sandra believed the engagement was based on love and affection, a ruse crafted by Cade, and Maureen abhorred deceiving her new friend. Did the end justify the means? Of course, she had had these feelings before, but never had it been this tough to accept her own actions, since she had plunged into this charade without thinking about the outcome and had taken for granted that she wouldn't be called accountable to Sandra. That had changed.

"What...what will you say to Sandra...when you tell her we've broken the engagement?" Maureen closed her eyes. "Oh, Lord, what am I going to say?"

He walked to a point beside her. "I'll take care of everything. You won't have to say a word."

"No way can I simply turn my back on her. She asked me to be her friend. And I want to be! For crying out loud, Cade, I *will* owe her an explanation.

"Don't worry about it. Maybe you won't have to..."

"Don't worry? How can I not? You and I..." Courage failed her, leaving her unable to verbalize her fears. Needing to collect her wits, Maureen yearned to take herself off to some private place, but she couldn't. If there were ever a moment when she and Cade needed to have an honest discussion, it was now.

Apparently he was of the same mind. "Looks like we've got several things to settle."

She inched her way into the pool's shallow end, the cold water biting all the way to her midriff as she gripped the edge. "Let's start with Sandra."

Feet first, Cade eased into the water and treaded in front of Maureen. "Let's don't. How she reacts is getting ahead of the problem. First, I want to get *our* situation settled."

Dread replaced her wretched guilt. But she shored up her dignity and squared her shoulders. "We've accomplished what we went after, as far as Sandra and Phil are concerned, so there's no need to go on with our phony engagement."

"Maybe, maybe not." He rested an elbow on the pool deck; his face was near Maureen's. "I'm not so certain their reconciliation is set in concrete—you heard her say they have problems to solve. I know her. The venerable Mrs. Uhr is a spoiled girl, and she may up and take another hike."

"What are you suggesting?"

"I think we ought to give them some time," he answered. "To make certain the reconciliation is real. In other words, I want us to go on being engaged. At least for another month or so. Besides, if we break up right now, everyone will be suspicious."

Cade wasn't telling her goodbye! Like a condemned man given a reprieve, Maureen gave a sigh of relief. But her conscience followed close behind.

Perhaps wanting reassurance, maybe needing for him to argue away her doubts, undoubtedly yearning for peace of mind, Maureen said, "It doesn't feel right. Before, she was your friend and your problem. Now she's my friend, too. I'm not so certain—"

His jaw tightening, he interrupted, "It's a little late to think of that. Why don't you do us both a favor? Spit out what you're trying to say. In a good one-syllable word. Do you, or do you not, want out?"

Not a sound passed her constricted throat.

"By your lack of reply, I take it to be yes," Cade said and glowered. "Dammit to hell, you're the most aggravating woman I've ever met in my life!"

Momentarily, her thoughts turned and she compressed her lips to keep from smiling. If nothing else, she had a special place in his thoughts.

His composure intact and blatantly cool, he faced Maureen. "Let me rephrase my offer. I've got too much invested in you to let you run away. You *will* stand good for your part of the contract. Got it?"

All matters but his arrogant demand left her mind. Anger surfaced, boiled, exploded. Her palm slapped the water, which stung, but she barely noticed the pain. "You've got too much *invested* in me? Yes, you've put out a wad of cash, but mostly it was for your father. As for the money expended on me, it is and always was a loan. A loan I've begun to repay and will retire as soon as possible!" Marshaling a modicum of calm, she reminded, "Furthermore, I have stood good for my end of the deal."

"There's more than one definition of invested."

"Spare me!"

She started away, but Cade grabbed her elbow, pulling her to him. His face was carved from something unmalleable and sharp; his eyes were rapiers; his fingers bit into her waist. "You want to call it quits, fine, do it. But you might want to think about what you're giving up. By the time your comely body is dry from this pool, I'll pull the plug on Wilburn Herrington."

Her fury reigning supreme, she raged, "I wouldn't put it past you. And I'm sure it wouldn't take your detective five minutes to find him, so—"

"You got that right. He'll find him, and I'll . . ."

Challenging this irritating, aggravating, infuriating *sidewinder* to act on the charge she didn't really mean, she fluttered her hand. "Pull your strings, pull the plug. No one's in a better position than the powerful Mr. Cade Herrington! Do it, go on, don't let anything stop you. Being who and what you are, decency toward a destitute parent won't ever enter your calculator brain!"

"You're trying to lay a guilt trip on me. It won't work, Maureen. You ought to know by now that I'm not susceptible."

"Right. You're not telling me anything I don't know already. You'll go to your grave hating the man who sired you. Well, it's your loss." She yanked away from Cade's strong fingers. "You asked me a minute ago if I wanted out of this little scheme of ours. I didn't answer you, but I will now. Yes, I want out. Want to know why?" She didn't give him a chance to answer. "I'm disgusted with your attitude. You malign your dad without giving him a chance to defend himself. Another thing. I'm tired of your playing God with Sandra's emotions. If she wants to be with Phil—or if she doesn't—that's her business, not yours or mine." Maureen swallowed a cough that threatened to interrupt her tirade. "If she makes a play for you, surely you're man enough to say, 'Sandra, I'm not going to marry you.' It's past time you gave her credit for character.''

"Finished?"

"No! I am sick of your *demands*. Since the moment I've had the displeasure of your company, you've ordered me to do this and that and the other! I am not your serf, Mr. Herrington. I am a woman who's done her level best to bring peace to two men. Two men in dire need of peace." She hugged her wet arms. "Furthermore, I never asked for your charity. You were the one who demanded I accept money and clothes. You demand, you expect—that's all you ever do!"

A strange gleam entered his dark eyes, and he rubbed his chin. "Anyone ever tell you you're cute when you're mad?"

She tightened her fists, her lips curling back. "How dare you fall to clichés at a moment like this!"

With that, she worked against the water pressure, making for the steps. Mission accomplished, dripping wet and mad as the proverbial wet hen, Maureen stomped toward the house. She was going to pack her bags.

The moment she huffed into her room, leaving Cade in her furious wake, trouble met her head-on.

Chapter Nine

Maureen, suddenly startled and apprehensive, pushed aside thoughts of Cade and their latest, most serious argument. She hurried across the bedroom rug. Fifi lay prone, beside the bed and with her breath coming in a rapid "Heh, heh, heh."

"What's wrong, kitty?"

Of course the cat couldn't answer, but she slapped Maureen's comforting hand, taking a minuscule shred of flesh and drawing an "Ouch!" from her rescuer. A weak hiss passed the fanged mouth. Her hackles matted as Fifi drew up her shoulders and gave a dry heave.

The illness's source became glaringly apparent when Maureen straightened to grant the cat some space. Shoved half under the bed was the box of cat snacks. What had been a full box was now empty, and a closer inspection of the underbed revealed a foil wrapper and a partially devoured chocolate bar. Fifi had ransacked the bedside table's open drawer; the sweet and the cat treats were now lining the marmalade cat's distended midsection.

"Oh, Fifi, you naughty girl." Maureen amended her castigation. "Fifi, I'm the naughty one for not closing the drawer."

Was overeating a threat to life? Surely not, she reasoned. She glanced at the crumpled wrapper, at the large and empty box, at the cat's bulging stomach. It looked like it might explode.

What am I going to do? Calling a vet seemed in order. But this was Cade's pet; she had to let him know about the situation. "That's just great, Feef," Maureen moaned, her sympathies not limited to the object of her words but also to herself. "After my big, dramatic exit scene, I've got to see his face. He has me so mad right now, I could wring his neck. And now...I've got to tell him I've foundered his cat."

Fifi belched, and Maureen rolled her eyes. "Enough is enough. You need a doctor."

On her way to fetch the cat carrier, she bumped into the source of her rage and dreams. Evidently a master at the quick change of clothes, he stood, arms akimbo, at the bottom of the stairs. She noted his Western boots, his jeans and a yoked shirt. But only for a split second.

"Leaving?" he asked, his face deceptively bland. "In your swimsuit, I might add."

"I'd leave naked if nec— Darn it, Cade! We don't have time for an argument! It's Fifi—she's upstairs in my room— she needs a doctor. I—"

"Settle down, settle down." His fingers slid to cup Maureen's shoulders. "What's wrong with the cat?"

"She ate a bunch of stuff. A box of treats and a candy bar."

"Where the hell did she..." His tone lightened. "You change clothes, I'll round her up."

At least he hadn't dressed her down about making the foodstuff available to the animal.

Following behind Cade's long strides, Maureen retraced her steps to the suite of rooms and hurried to the bathroom. She was dressed in an economy of motions, her fingers providing a brush for her damp and weighty hair. Charging into the sleeping area, she watched Cade lift the cat carrier in one hand and offer her a piece of paper with the other.

His eyes were moving over Maureen. Was that sadness or perhaps regret reflected in those eyes?

"The maid took a message for you," he said. "Did you see it?"

She waved a dismissive hand. "I didn't."

"You'll be interested to know your insurance adjuster called. Looks like your claim against the fire is being settled."

Presently a burned-out home and factory were the least of Maureen's concerns. She rammed the message into her shorts pocket. "I'll think about it after we've gotten Fifi taken care of."

Cade and Maureen didn't speak another syllable during the short drive to New Braunfels, to the office of Garry Wellmann, DVM. After the veterinarian had asked the appropriate questions, he sent the cat owner and his concerned companion to an empty waiting room, saying, "I need to get our little friend comfortable."

Amid antiseptic smells mingled with the fume of animals, Maureen sat down on a vinyl couch. Cade grabbed a brochure on obesity in felines, then took the chair to Maureen's left. Intent on his study, he read through the pamphlet.

"Cade, about Fifi, I—"

"The cat's going to be all right, Maureen. Quit worrying." He placed his reading material back on the shelf. "Don't you want to read your note from the insurance people? I didn't tell you all of it."

She extracted the scrap of paper from her shorts pocket, but there was no way she could focus on the lettering. "To be honest, Cade, I'm too upset to read it. What else does it say?" She pushed the note across the couch, in his direction.

But he didn't need a reminder. "They'll be cutting you a check next week."

"That's nice. I can settle with the landlord. And with you."

"That's not—"

His reply was interrupted as the doors separating the waiting room from the clinical area swung open. The veterinarian said, "Your cat will be fine, Mr. Herrington, but I'd like to keep her here overnight."

Comforted by the prognosis, Maureen heaved a sigh. Yet her nerves were as jagged as a serrated knife. So many things had happened over the past twenty-four hours, some good, some bad, but the worst had been the poolside situation with Cade. Although the proud urge to pack the belongings she had brought to the Dry Hole Ranch, to leave Cade and repay every cent he had invested still occupied her mind, she wasn't averse when he suggested they take a walk through Landa Park.

The nearby, sprawling park, which had been given to the city by a 19th century German-Jewish immigrant to New Braunfels, had lush foliage, crystal springs and recreational facilities. Maureen and Cade avoided the more populated areas, opting for the quiet of sheltering trees and rich St. Augustine grass. A mockingbird flew from one tree to another as they strolled across the grounds, a few feet distancing them in space, an indeterminable gulf parting them in spirit.

He made the first move to bridge the gap. He pointed to the mockingbird and said conversationally, "Lovely sound, isn't it?"

"Yes."

"Do you like the outdoors?"

"Very much so."

"I'm sorry to say there are a lot of things I don't know about you." He stopped to snap a small limb from a live-oak tree. "And there are a lot of things I wish I'd found out before you decided to leave me."

What could she say? *Oh, gee, Cade, how kind of you to have regrets,* or *Golly, I thought your investigator found out everything about me.* Right then she wasn't certain of her mind-set, but she admitted inwardly that his admission was working against the anger she wanted to hold.

Into the silence, Cade said, "That message in your pocket—" a forefinger motioned toward her Bermuda shorts "—mentions something besides the payoff." Tossing the limb aside, he squinted at the tent of leaves above his head, then pushed his thumbs behind his shiny silver belt buckle. "The insurance investigator has pinned down the cause of the fire. The oven was defective. The 220 wiring had nothing to do with the cause."

"Then, Wilburn wasn't to—" She clamped her mouth. Getting into another argument, especially one centered around the elder Herrington, was the last thing she wanted.

"If you were going to say my father isn't to blame, you're absolutely right." Cade captured Maureen's elbows. "Honey, I was wrong to blame him. Dead wrong. And I'm sorry for hurting you and maligning him. I owe you both an apology."

"I never thought I'd hear you— Oh, Cade, you're quite a man."

His apology dissolved the last vestiges of her anger, and the mockingbird's sweet song matched the sudden trill in her heart. For the first time, she felt as if there was a chance for a reconciliation between Cade and his father. Granted, hope was small, but she would take her hopes wherever they were found.

She reassessed all that had transpired at poolside. She had screamed a lot of things at him, words that she regretted for the most part. Most of all, she yearned to make amends with Cade.

He made the first move. "I've been wrong about a lot of things." His hands caressed her arms. "Maureen, if I ask you something, will you promise to hear me out . . . without interrupting?"

"I suppose I'm capable."

"My turn to give thanks," he said wryly, before turning serious again. "I wouldn't have gone through with my threat. You've more than done your part in our engagement deal, so you've earned Wilburn's money."

She opened her mouth, but Cade gave no opportunity for her comment. He said, "About those things you accused me of this morning—I'm guilty of them, too. I have done a lot of expecting and demanding. I should've employed the polite request."

"I was unfair, too," Maureen told him. "I'm in no position to make demands, myself. You've been nothing but generous with me. Actually, I think you're the most generous person in the world."

Fair and truly complimented, Cade smiled. "I do my best, and I didn't mean to offend you when I used the word 'invested.' Wrong choice of words."

"Mine weren't very fair, either. I was upset, thinking about what Sandra's reaction will be if and when she learns the truth." Maureen gave thought to the matter of Uhr and Uhr, a subject she had refused to mull until this moment, and she came to a conclusion. "You were right. If we break up now, it'll draw suspicion to our motives."

His eyes widened. "*If* we break up? I thought you'd decided we were past tense."

She swallowed. She stared into those questioning dark eyes. Just looking at him roused a passion in Maureen, the desire to melt into the depths of his soul and be in his long, strong arms forever and ever and ever. Not a new emotion.

By now Maureen would have promised her firstborn to gypsy peddlers for another chance with Cade. "Is your offer still open?" she asked and held her breath.

He stepped back, then strode over to stop beside a narrow stream. Bending at the knee, he rocked back on his heels and rested an elbow on his leg. What was he thinking? she wondered. Was it too late to mend fences between the two of them?

At last, he returned to Maureen's side. "Yeah, the offer's still good."

Tension eased in her heart, and she smiled. "I'm glad."

"Let's get back to the ranch. I want to call my attorney."

"Your attorney? Why?"

"To transfer the Cutter's Mill property to your name."

What? She must have gotten water in her ears this morning. He wanted to *give* her the gristmill?

Surely he didn't. Cade was the most generous person she had ever known, but business was business.

When he said, "I want to make absolutely certain we don't have a repeat of this morning," she realized she had heard him right.

A while back, during her first visit to his ranch, he had mentioned that everyone could be bought, provided the right price was negotiated. She had to make him understand that neither her heart nor her principles had a price tag.

"When Cutter's Mill becomes mine," she said, "it'll be because I've paid for it. I don't want it as a gift. I want to go with our original agreement."

"You're saying you don't want me to give you the property?" he asked, astounded.

"That's right."

Was it the sun lighting his amber eyes, or did the brightness stem from his soul? Whatever the case, he was like a man who had just hit a winning homer in the World Series. Cade crushed her to him, planted a hard kiss on her lips and twirled her around.

"Damned if you aren't the most amazing woman I've ever met!"

Previously she had been the most aggravating woman he had ever met, and Maureen supposed that was still so. But "amazing" was a nice addition to her dubious claim.

When Cade and Maureen returned to the ranch, a problem arose that had nothing to do with the usual. The politics of oil. Douglas Smythe informed Cade, "Jake's thrown his hat in the ring. He's going for the PPA presidency."

Cade met the news with steely determination to win the seat for himself. Thus began two hectic weeks. At his suggestion, they attended every social function remotely related to the petroleum community. During these busy days and nights, he treated Maureen with all respect, and she returned his gestures. Furthermore, there was a confidence to him that she hadn't detected before. At last, she felt as if he trusted her.

And it was a marvelous feeling.

Yet . . . he kept his guard about some unspoken problem, as if he were trying to settle his mind about something. As usual, he offered no insights, and Maureen pegged his preoccupation as preelection jitters. Jake Patton was conducting an expensive and tireless campaign for the presidency, and Cade had to be on his toes. Capturing the post for himself seemed to be his most ardent desire.

Which troubled Maureen. His wanting the presidency's responsibilities and prestige didn't bother her. But his close attention to the election reminded her of his reason for running—to prove he could best his father.

Wilburn. She still hadn't heard from him. In that light, she didn't mention the weekend get-together that had been a large part of her reason for agreeing to the engagement sham.

Then, a fortnight before the annual PPA elections dinner, fortune frowned on Fortuna Enterprises.

Cade's corporation was producing oil off the coast of Brazil, and the native workers called a strike. Labor problems forced him, along with Douglas Smythe and a planeload of their personnel, to go to South America. Two days after they departed, Cade telephoned Maureen and told her it was doubtful he'd return in time for the election results.

The next day, in the halcyon hour of predusk, she rode Sadie across the ridge below the ranch house. A car horn blared twice, and she reined in to the sound. His beat-up Pontiac shining like a star, Wilburn stepped out of his car and onto the circular driveway.

Maureen tapped her heel to the mare's powerful flank and hurried to the stable. Handing Sadie's reins to a ranch hand, she rushed into the den.

Where her stepfather was beaming.

"We did it, Sugar Pie! Texas Bakeries is going to buy those licensing rights!"

Wilburn bounded across the room and whirled Maureen into his arms, as if she didn't smell like perspiration and horse. Round and round, he whirled her until her head was spinning. All the while, he laughed with joy. His actions were so like Cade's, she thought, recalling the moment she had informed him that Cutter's Mill wasn't for renegotiation. Not only did the Herrington men bear a physical resemblance, they also shared a like exuberance during times of obvious delight.

"Granny Miniver's Famous is going to be a brand of Texas Bakeries!" Wilburn exclaimed.

The news should have given her instant euphoria—she'd achieved her professional goal—yet her feelings were mixed. Gently, she pulled away. "Is that where you've been all this time, courting them?"

"Not the entire time."

His eyes gleamed with pride and accomplishment, and she couldn't stay angry at his silence of late. "Don't keep me in suspense," she prompted.

"They're offering the world."

He named a figure that sent her senses soaring.

"A couple of the VPs will be down here Monday to finalize the transaction," Wilburn said. "By that afternoon, all the money will be in your bank account."

She would be in a position to exercise the option on Cutter's Mill; she had the finances to equip it and hire employees. She was rich!

She couldn't wait to tell Cade.

"Sugar Pie, that's not all." Grinning, Wilburn reached into his pocket and presented a white card. "Read it."

She did. "W. Herrington Fittings of Midland, Texas. Wilburn Herrington, President."

"That's me."

"Then you... Did you do something with Cade's design?"

"You bet I did. Hired a machinist—fellow I knew and trusted—and he and I worked on it night and day. When I wasn't jawing with those bakery folks, that is. Anyway, we revved up that beauty last week, and it works like a dream." He winked. "Been beating the concrete, too, Sugar Pie. I'm selling reconditioned couplings, quick as we can fix 'em." He pulled a check from his shirt pocket, placing it on the coffee table. "That there's the fifty thousand Cade advanced me."

She reached to hug his shoulders and kiss his weathered cheek. "I'm so happy for you! Congratulations."

"Pretty pleased, myself, if I do say so." Wilburn, his feet light as air, made for the sofa and sat down.

She walked to the sliding doors. A quarter minute passed before she faced him again. "You do have a right to be proud, but I think you were unfair not to keep in touch with me. It wasn't right, and not like you at all."

Wilburn bent forward, resting his elbows on his knees. "I had my reasons, and you ought to recall 'em. When I left here, I promised to make the both of you proud of me, and I didn't want to be making... I don't know—progress reports? I *needed* for everything to be... well, a success. Can you understand that, Maureen?"

"Yes, I can," she answered honestly. "But I've had all kinds of awful thoughts about you. For all I knew, you could've been lying dead in some ditch. You could've taken off with Cade's design. You could've—"

Wilburn's face fell. "Have you lost faith in me?" He rubbed his eyes. "Cade's been talking to you."

"Yes. He told me..." She swallowed. "He said you were unfaithful to his mother. But I don't believe him."

"Believe him. It's..." He pushed to his feet, his back straight. "It's true."

Disgusted, disquieted, disappointed, Maureen gasped before shock beset her, rendering her incapable of speech.

"I made a lot of mistakes in my younger years, Maureen. Too many mistakes to count. Still make them, but not like the earlier ones. The, uh, unfaithful part was a once and stupid thing. By the time I realized what I'd done...it was too late to make amends. My family was lost to me.

"But you've known me a dozen years, Maureen. You know I haven't given up wanting to settle matters between me and Cade. I need to atone for my sins. It's just that..." He stared at the floor. "I don't know how to go about it. There's so much I...I can't say about the situation."

"To me? Or to Cade?"

"To both of you."

"If there's something that needs airing, you shouldn't hold back. Whatever it is, it's keeping you and your son apart."

He raked his hand through his mane of gray hair, but didn't offer a reply.

Maureen refused to let the matter drop. Too much rode on his honesty. She pondered his admissions, and arrived at the only conclusion she could draw. "What drove you to another woman?"

A hush fell over the den, lightened only by the grandfather clock. Wilburn walked to the sideboard and poured himself a stiff drink. He quaffed the bourbon, set the glass down and squinted at the ceiling.

His eyes leveling hers, Wilburn replied, "I drove myself to infidelity."

"I imagine that sort of thing isn't one-sided, in some cases. Knowing you, I'd imagine Rowena did something to turn you away."

"That would be the coward's way, Maureen, blaming her. I won't do that."

"Then, will you tell me about Rowena? I always thought she was awful...until Frieda Wittig said she wasn't. I don't know what to believe."

"She was a good woman, kind and generous and loving."

"And you turned to another woman," Maureen pointed out, disgust etching her words. "You had a lot of gall taking Pemberton money."

"I didn't."

Maureen listened to his tone, watched his expression, and she had no difficulty believing him.

"But Cade thinks you absconded with the money." She ran her palms down her slacks. "You should tell him that wasn't the case."

"No."

"Why not? I think it would make a difference... maybe...if he knew.... He's got a thing about money and the price of one's principles."

"I'll never tell him. And don't you, either!"

"Why not?"

"I have my reasons."

"Listen, I think I have a right to know."

"Maureen, this is between me and my boy."

She was *not* going to leave this room until she got the truth. "It concerns me, too. I love Cade very much. I'd like to think someday we'll have a permanent relationship. But until the two of you air your differences, that will never happen. He thinks you sold out, then his first love rejected him. For the love of the almighty dollar." Maureen massaged her suddenly aching temples. "For God's sake, he needs the truth from you. *I* need the truth."

Wilburn stepped to the sliding-glass doors and shoved his fingers into his back pockets. He stared at the countryside for a long moment. Rubbing his hand down his face, he groaned and turned to Maureen.

"One night Rowena and I had an argument. I don't even remember what it was about, it was such a silly, insignificant thing. I stomped out of the house and figured I'd find a friendly ear down at the corner beer joint. Place was closed for some reason. So, I drove to my office. My secretary showed up. She'd forgotten to take care of the mail that afternoon. I, uh, I'd rather not go into the details of the rest."

"Better you don't. I don't need a description. Just the facts."

"Rowena found us."

"Can you blame her for demanding a divorce?"

"No, I never did. But I wanted to patch things up. Oh, God, Maureen, it's so easy to make a mistake and it's so difficult to live with it!"

And Wilburn had had two decades to regret his weakness. Twenty years—most of her life. And sometimes she felt as if she had been on this earth for a hundred years. What had it been like for him? She saw it all in the tired lines of his face. He had never forgiven himself, nor had he given up hope of being forgiven. His was a private hell.

It wasn't her place to forgive—that belonged to the departed Rowena and to Cade—but Maureen felt her stepfather had paid a high enough price for his transgression.

She crossed the hooked rug to close her fingers around his life-roughened hand. "Maybe you shouldn't say any more."

"You wanted to know—" he squeezed her hand "—and maybe I need to finish, now that I've gotten started."

Maureen had asked for honesty, and though it was uncomfortable being privy to dark secrets, this was no time for a faint heart. "What happened after Rowena discovered you, um, you know...?"

"She said she'd call the newspapers if I didn't go along with her terms. I wasn't scared of a scandal, but I didn't want my boy to suffer for my sin. So I agreed to the divorce and signed away my visitation rights to Cade."

"But the story got to him that you'd taken what wasn't rightfully yours."

"That's the way the story goes."

"What's the true one?"

"She set out to poison his mind against me."

Maureen grimaced. "She succeeded."

"Yes, and Rowena wanted more revenge. As soon as I'd signed away my life, she called a newspaper reporter. By the next morning I was ruined in the oil business. 'Course, a lot of those ole boys have gone to a greater reward now," he added, trying to infuse levity. "On this go-around, though, thanks to time and your faith and my son's loan, I'm making it big."

Making it big. Cade had done that. And he still had his aspirations. Maureen gave thought to his motivation for gaining the PPA presidency. He had said it had something to do with bringing honor to the Herrington name. Now she knew exactly what he meant.

Further, she sympathized with his reasoning.

"Cade needs to know the truth about what Rowena did to you," Maureen said.

"No."

"Give me one good reason why not."

"I won't have him knowing his mother could be mean and spiteful. Their relationship was the only good one he's ever had with a woman, and—"

"You haven't been around him, so how do you know that?"

"Rowena told me so." Wilburn took a heaving breath. "She called me to the hospital when she was dying and asked if we could make peace." He glanced at the ceiling, then at Maureen. "She asked me to make peace with him, too. Rowena wanted to tell him the truth, herself."

"Why didn't she?"

Wilburn's eyes brimmed with tears. "She passed away while I was holding her hand."

Maureen cried, too. She cried for a shattered home, for a woman who had waited too late to reap the benefits of a settled conscience...and for Cade. He had lost both parents, one through Wilburn's mistakes, the other through death, and in the aftermath, he had spent miserable years.

Wilburn folded his arms around Maureen, and she felt his shudders. "She wanted me to tell him, but I can't be honest," he said, choking out the words. "He'd figure I deserved what I got. And I do. But more than anything, he might begin to accept the truth. If he did, it would hurt him."

"How?"

"By knowing she'd done those vengeful things. Let him keep her on a pedestal. I'm willing to pay the consequences."

"You've paid enough," Maureen replied. "Somehow, some way, you and Cade will be reunited."

Chapter Ten

On the heel of his confession, Wilburn returned to Midland, leaving Maureen at the ranch with her doubts. Should she tell Cade the truth about his parents? She eventually decided to honor Wilburn's wish. Cade didn't need to know about his mother's dark side.

Some things were better left unsaid.

Once he returned from South America, Maureen knew she'd have plenty to say to Cade. Confessing her love would be the main topic. How would he react? And what would he say about the check from W. Herrington Fittings? Surely he'd be proud of his father's recent success, and the men could go on from there.

She'd have another check to tell him about—the whopping one from Texas Bakeries that she had deposited in her bank account. But as the days passed, she began to worry over announcing the good news.

Beyond his request to continue their ruse, she had no excuse to stay in his household, now that she was financially secure. From the start, her plan had been to unite father and son through a business arrangement. That hadn't worked. Wilburn had been successful without Cade's personal intervention.

The only thing holding Cade and Maureen together was her love and the tentativeness of the Uhr marriage.

Even that slim thread snapped when Sandra stopped by the ranch to inform Maureen that everything was going smoothly for the Uhrs. Now Cade would have no reason to continue the engagement ruse. Unless he returned Maureen's love....

On the afternoon of the PPA elections dinner, the telephone rang.

"Hello there, Blue Eyes, this is the South American connection," Maureen heard Cade say. "I'm in the good old U.S. of A.—Miami, to be exact."

His easy tone and the sound of his voice drew a smile from her. "Welcome back. Looks like you'll be here in time for the election results."

"Yeah, but you'll have to meet me at the Derrick Club. We've got a mechanical problem with the plane, so I'm catching a commercial flight home. Make that *flights,* since I'll have to change planes in Houston. I'll catch up with you around nine this evening."

"I'll be counting the hours."

"Me, too."

There was promise in those two words! Or was he just antsy to get to the Derrick Club? By gosh, she would find out. Tonight. At the first opportunity.

"By the way, Cade, I have some good news. Your father was here a few days ago. He's been a busy man. Your invention is a marvel, and he's been selling reconditioned couplings as fast as he can turn them out." She waited in vain for a positive response. "He left you a check for fifty thousand dollars," she added.

"That's nice."

"Nice? It's wonderful! He's making a success of himself."

"Look, I've got to go. They're calling my plane. See you tonight."

He broke the connection.

Maureen spent the rest of the afternoon feeling disappointed that he hadn't shown more enthusiasm over his father's strides. But maybe he had been in a rush for the plane and would show some interest once he returned to San Antonio.

She held on to that hope as she dressed for the evening, taking extra care with her appearance. The man she loved would be home tonight. She ached to see him.

The Derrick Club, bastion of the oil elite, was resplendent in mauve and blue. The ballroom was filled to capacity with oilmen and their women.

Nine o'clock passed.

Food had been cleared from the tables. Smooth as Lamborghinis on a super highway, waiters wound through the crowd to present after-dinner libations. Ed Hamcek's dance band—all members past middle age and their music showing it—filled the air with strains of Benny Goodman. And Maureen, sitting at a table with Sandra and Phil, toyed with her coffee cup. Where was Cade?

She tried not to think about airplane mechanical problems. Surely his plane was just delayed, that was all.

In less than ten minutes, the current PPA president would announce the election returns. After all his hard work to win the presidency, it would be a shame for Cade to miss his victory. And Maureen was certain of his success. She had every confidence that he would become the organization's next leader.

She eyed Cade's opponent, who sat at the next table. Unlike his usual self, Jake Patton didn't hog the conversation with his tablemates; he wasn't saying a word and his features were strained. Obviously this election meant as much to him as it did to Cade, and election jitters had gotten to him.

Pamela, Maureen observed, was just as nervous, but her anxieties were directed at her husband. There was loving concern in her actions. *She loves that oaf. Maybe she always did. Maybe she married him for love, not money.* Stranger things had happened.

Heads began to turn toward the ballroom's entrance. Murmurs and clapping hands announced Cade's arrival. Maureen sighed in relief.

From a distance, she took in his tuxedo. He looked marvelous, as usual. Several people stopped him as he made his way toward Maureen's table, but he didn't tarry.

On closer observation she saw tiredness in his dark eyes, weariness in his strong features, when he leaned to kiss her. "You look gorgeous...and I've missed you," he whispered in her ear, a tendril of his breath dancing against her neck and drawing a shiver of delight. Her fingers slid to the back of his head, guiding his mouth to the lips that showed how much she had missed him.

"Break it up, break it up," Phil Uhr ordered lightly. "Can't have an X-rated show. Might get the folks so excited, they'd make a mad exodus for—"

"Hush, Cupcake." Sandra touched a French-manicured forefinger to her husband's lips. "You ought to know better than to interrupt a welcome-home embrace."

Nonetheless, the kiss was interrupted. Cade gently squeezed Maureen's shoulder, took the seat next to hers and greeted the Uhrs. His palm found her thigh; she covered his hand with her own. His eyes never abandoned Maureen, and he stared at her as if trying to drink in her presence. Reveling in his nearness, in the emotion he telegraphed, she knew...

She knew he loved her.

Her heart took wings, and she smiled.

"Where's my father?" Sandra asked.

"Still in Brazil. After we finished negotiating the new contract, he decided to spend some time at Ipanema."

"Well, darn." A petulant frown bowed Sandra's mouth. "Phil and I were hoping he'd be back before we went to—" a grin replaced the frown "—Maui."

"Isn't that where you spent your honeymoon?" Cade asked.

Phil's chest puffed. "Yes... and that's where we'll be spending the second one. We leave tomorrow."

Beaming, Cade said, "It's about time."

"We knew you'd be pleased." In mock aggravation, Sandra waved a finger at Maureen. "Naughty girl, I thought you would've told Cade all about it."

"International phone calls are expensive," Maureen hedged. "And I thought he'd want to hear it from you."

Cade riveted a questioning look her way. She knew he had to be wondering *why* she hadn't told him. She should have.

The microphone squeaked, drawing attention to the podium.

"Ladies and gentlemen, may I have your attention, please?" The association president held an envelope. He broke the seal as Ed Hamcek's percussionist began a drum roll. "We have a new president. Cade Herrington, stand up and take a bow!"

Maureen's eardrum vibrated at a bellowed "No!"

Cade glanced at the next table, a look of pity in his eyes. But he didn't belabor it. He hugged her, then rose to his feet, a smile of satisfaction, of relief, of victory in his expression. It was as if he had been given a prize of huge proportions, such as winning the United States presidency, and Maureen was thrilled for him.

The next few seconds whirred by. Droves of Cade's peers offered felicitations. But they backed away. A man's form cast a huge shadow as he lumbered toward the president-elect's table. Maureen drew in her breath. Would Jake make a scene?

Cade extended his hand.

Slowly, like treacle on a winter's day, Jake lifted his arm. Then a genuine smile cut across the giant's doughy features, and he grabbed and pumped the offered make-peace. His free hand went to slap the winner's back. "I did my best to beat ya, boy, but you've proved yourself, and I want you to know—you've got my support."

While Maureen exhaled, Cade said earnestly, "And you've got mine, Jake. We need to run this organization with mutual cooperation. And I appreciate yours."

Pamela stepped next to her husband, and he put his arm around her waist. "You know, Herrington, you've been a good example to me. Last July Fourth, when you and your lady had me and mine over for dinner, I got to thinking. If you can take time away from work to get hitched and have a honeymoon, I can take time for my family. Pammie here, she's been wanting to take one of those balloon trips through the Loire Valley, but I said no. I was too busy." He hugged his wife closer to his side. "Changed my mind, though. We're leaving next week on our *first* honeymoon."

Maureen chuckled with irony. The sham had worked wonders beyond getting the Uhrs back together.

Cade grinned. "Don't keep too far out of touch, Jake. If you want it, the chairmanship of the Advisory Council is yours."

Jake's tiny eyes widened in surprise—and pleasure. "You bet I want it."

"Looks like we've all got a bright future ahead of us," Cade commented.

Again, the announcer took the microphone. "Cade Herrington, we're waiting for your acceptance speech. And you've got a photo session. Get on up here!"

Jake and Pamela retook their chairs, as did Maureen and the Uhrs, while Cade strode to the podium. His words were short and to the point, drawing cheers. The photographer started his duties, and Ed Hamcek lifted his baton. Butchered chords of a rock song began. And Maureen gave a prayer of thanks.

Having Jake's support would help Cade in his organizational duties. Further, she felt that the two men might someday be friends. Could she hope that Cade would someday view his father as more than an adversary?

"Isn't life grand?" Sandra asked, yanking Maureen to the present. "Everything's falling into place."

Not everything, Sandra. Cade has his office, Jake accepted his loss, and you and Phil have each other. But what happens next between me and Cade? And with Wilburn?

"Aren't you pleased for Cade?"

"Of course I am." Maureen picked up her evening bag. "Excuse me. I need to powder my nose."

Powdering her nose was an excuse for fresh air. Maureen exited the ballroom, circumvented the doormen and stepped outdoors. She stopped near the building corner, under the light of a security lamp.

Sandra followed. Worried concern touched her delicate features, and she asked, "Something's troubling you. Would you like to talk?"

Maureen would have welcomed a friendly ear, but there was no way she could express fears to Sandra. "Everything's over," she allowed, "and I'm ready to unravel."

The blonde misunderstood. "The election was difficult. And you've had the added stress of a romance."

"Stress of a romance?"

"All romances are stressful. Will he? Won't he? Will she? Won't she? That sort of stuff. To tell the truth, I've been concerned about you and Cade. Sometimes there's a certain tension between the two of you. You know, like you're scared of each other."

Obviously they hadn't played their parts as well as Maureen had thought. "I don't think Cade is scared of anything."

"He's as vulnerable as the next guy. Cade has a fear of losing. Just like when he threw his hat into this election ring. He wanted the presidency in the worst way, and Dad and I thought he'd go to any lengths to win it."

"That is Cade's way."

Shuttering her eyes, Sandra tugged her bottom lip between her teeth. One hand rubbed the other. At last she said, "Do you think we're good enough friends—Maureen, can I be honest with you?"

"Absolutely."

"In the beginning...did you and Cade have some sort of arrangement? What I mean is... Dad and I couldn't help but think... Well, your courtship was so whirlwind, and you did profit in your business—awfully soon after the fire. Don't get me wrong, I know you and Cade are going to get married, but..."

Maureen felt a blush spreading to her face.

"But we assumed you and Cade had some sort of business arrangement," Sandra continued, "since..."

And when she had finished expressing her doubts, Maureen's blush turned ashen. *It can't be true. Cade wouldn't—*

"Oh, Maureen, I'm so sorry." Sandra took her hand. "I never dreamed you didn't know."

Maureen didn't utter six words in the aftermath of Sandra's startling yet artless revelations. When she and Cade arrived at the Dry Hole and entered the living area for his suggested nightcap, she asked woodenly, "Did you..." Please let him deny it, she prayed. "Did you need a wife, or the promise of one, to win the PPA presidency? Is that why you wanted this crazy engagement of ours?"

Cade's hand stalled over the ice bucket. He slowly took a swig of his drink. "Not on your life."

She wanted to believe him. But couldn't. Was it because of the funny look on his tanned features? Or was it the way he swallowed his words along with the bourbon and water?

"I hope you're being honest, Cade." He refused to meet Maureen's eyes, and his action confirmed her suspicions. "I'm going for a walk," she announced, feeling as if the walls were closing in on her.

"How 'bout I join you?"

"No thank you."

She left the room and went for a change of clothes. Wearing cotton slacks, a scooped-neck pullover and sneakers, she faced the night air. For twenty, maybe thirty minutes she walked the path leading away from the house. Not a cloud obstructed the midnight sky... all the clouds were in her heart.

By the stream, she slowed her pace and sat down to listen to the gurgle of water. Other sounds entered her ears—

hoofbeats, a horse neighing, a man's voice calling her name. She hugged her knees as horse and rider approached. Then she heard the saddle creak as a familiar form eased from it. Titan snorted, and Cade patted the stallion's head before tethering the reins to a tree branch. She stared at the ground.

"I lied to you."

Maureen's head snapped up at Cade's admission.

"The PPA presidency had a lot to do with why I wanted you to pose as my fiancée," he said. "Not everything, but a lot."

Her equanimity rocked by his lie of omission, she didn't know whether to laugh or cry, to scream or to say nothing. But she realized Cade wasn't the man she had fallen in love with. All along she had figured his whole motivation behind the engagement package had been generous and giving and admirable.

A voice in her brain reminded Maureen that she was keeping things back, too. Like the true story of his parents. Which she would never tell. Like selling the rights to Granny Miniver's Famous. Right now, though, she was too hurt and disappointed to make explanations.

"Pardon my curiosity, but how big a role did Sandra's happiness really play in your scheme?" she asked.

"The biggest."

"A lot and the biggest add up to more than a hundred percent."

"Maybe I wanted more than a hundred percent. Maybe I wanted to win the election, for Sandra to find herself, for you to—" His voice was quiet, pained. "I made a mistake, not being frank with you."

Mistake—the word echoed through her head. Yes, Cade had made a wrong move. He hadn't told her his entire reason for wanting her cooperation in the charade. His misjudgment didn't come close to Wilburn's mistakes, though.

Her head throbbed. "I'm making too much of it, I know," she said. "You had a hard trip from South America and a big evening at the PPA. You must be tired. I know I am," she added honestly. "A good night's sleep will do us both good."

She started down the path leading to the house. Cade, leading Titan, stopped next to her.

"Lady, may I give you a lift?"

Despite her roiling emotions, despite her throbbing head that screamed for solitude, she didn't refuse the offer.

She put her foot in the stirrup, and Cade's hand supported her derriere as she threw a leg over the saddle. Grasping the pommel, she arched her back and faced forward. And when Cade settled behind her, she inched toward the saddle horn.

He clicked his tongue, and the stallion set a course for the ranch house. Cade took the reins in one hand and with the other, he swept the curtain of hair from her neck. She felt his lips feather her nape, and a frisson of excitement curled through her spine.

"Will you forgive me?" he asked. "I didn't set out to lie to you about the PPA."

Right then, she would have forgiven him anything.

Chapter Eleven

With Titan stabled, Cade escorted Maureen to her bedroom door. He brought her fingers to his lips. "Thanks for forgiving me." Her reply was to cup his face and move against him. He groaned in delight, his fingers curling on her shoulders. "You're everything I've ever wanted in a woman," he whispered.

She sighed. Those words were next to an open declaration of love. And they were wonderful, marvelous, stupendous! "Oh, Cade, my darling, I love you!"

His whoop of joy rang through the upstairs hallway. He whirled her around; her feet almost contacted the wall. But physical safety? That was far from her spinning mind. All she could think about was Cade!

The sweet moment he ceased his exuberant actions, he splayed his fingers across her back. His body molded to hers, and the heat of desire flamed between them. He kissed her. She kissed him. His fingers caressed, hers explored. In the conflagration of loving passion, she had never been so happy, so secure.

His lips nuzzled the lobe of her ear. "If we don't stop this, we'll be in that bedroom, and it's not right. Yet."

"It's right enough for me" was her murmured reply.

"Sweetheart, there's something… Wait right here. I'll be back in a flash."

"Where are you going?"

Putting two fingers to her lips, he commanded, "Shh."

He strutted down the hall, down the stairs and out of Maureen's sight. She shook her head in bewildered happiness. Whatever he was about, it had to be good.

She waited in the bedroom.

The window seat, her favorite place in this room, beckoned, and she curled up on it. Her heart in rhythm with soaring love, she smiled. The future was theirs.

She heard a thump and purring vibration, as Fifi crawled onto her lap.

"Hi there, Feef. Wonder what your master's up to?"

The cat's big, jade-colored eyes stared into Maureen's blue ones.

"What's taking him so long?"

Fifi licked her paw, then fastened an evil eye on the human. *Don't be impatient* was the message Maureen read.

"Well, I am impatient. This waiting is worse than when he was a continent away."

But wait she did. Five minutes. Ten. Fifteen. At the point of exasperation, she stood. It was then that she heard his footsteps on the stairs. But they weren't mere footsteps, those were the sounds of anger.

What had gone wrong?

Fury dyeing his amber eyes to black, Cade charged into her bedroom and slammed the door behind him. Fifi ran for cover. Maureen swallowed.

"I went downstairs to get this." He tossed a small box on the bedspread. "It's a ring. An engagement ring. One that was made to order without a stigma attached to it."

"I—I don't understand," she said honestly, disoriented by his change of mood.

"Let me give it to you straight, then." His voice held a rapier's edge. "I had the ring made in Brazil, had it shipped to my office. My secretary sent it out here. Along with a pile of press clippings. Interesting, what a man learns when he returns from out of country. Seems as if a certain cookie maker by the name of Miniver has sold out to Texas Bakeries."

Her mouth was so dry, she could barely choke out, "Yes, I did."

"Nice of you to tell me, Maureen."

"I—I w-wanted to tell you—"

"That so? Funny, I seem to recall a phone conversation and a few opportunities tonight. Not a word passed your lips."

"If I'd told you, you wouldn't've had a reason to stay with me. I made a mistake, I know."

"A mistake? Or a well-thought-out move? You've done a lot of that here lately. You've been manipulating me since day one. Except, I was too blind to see it. You're no different from Pam or that scoundrel who calls himself my father. You're greedy."

"I don't deserve that," she lashed out, angry that he didn't trust her enough to grant the benefit of a doubt.

"What do you deserve, Maureen? I shouldn't give a damn enough to care, but before I get the hell out of here, I'd like to know what you thought you had coming the morning you charged into my office."

While her pride screamed to throw his curses back at him, Maureen gathered calm. If she could just convince him she hadn't been devious, he might do some calming down, too.

"When I asked you to help your father, I thought if you were involved with him in a business partnership, you two would be together. The money wasn't what I was after. All I wanted to do was be a peacemaker of sorts. And, yes, I accepted money for the cookie factory, but if you'll think back on it, I didn't want your help. You were the one who demanded I take it. And I've been repaying the *loan*."

"Granted, you're a good credit risk. But I recall you wouldn't agree to our business arrangement until I promised to option Cutter's Mill to you."

"I was on the brink of saying yes when the gristmill became part of the scenario, so I . . ." She faced the window, hugging her arms, and tried to form the right words. If there was a chance for them to share a future, she had to be forthright. "Cade, I'm not going to whitewash it. Cutter's Mill had a lot to do with my decision to say yes. I wanted that place in the worst way, and my motives were strictly selfish along that line."

She heard his footsteps retracing a path to the door, and she turned to half face him. His back to Maureen, he planted one hand high on the door frame, the other at his side. "I know that," he said in a ragged voice. "I always knew it. But my foolish heart convinced my better judgment that you were a woman without a price tag."

"I don't have a price tag." She walked up to his rigid back and put her hand on his shoulder. "There's no price on my principles. Or my feelings."

"Now that's rich." His chuckle was devoid of humor. "And pardon me if I don't agree. You're like all the rest, eager to sell out to the highest bidder. And in your case, you thought you'd found him. *Me.* You've been enjoying the good life, baby. Don't think I haven't noticed it. Take that ring on your finger, for example. You put up a big fuss about wearing it, yet I haven't seen it off your finger.''

"You're right. It's still on my hand.'' Patience was one thing; allowing herself to become a victim was another. She hitched up her chin. "After everyone had seen me wear it, what could I do? You bought it for show, and I—''

"I didn't buy it entirely for show. Even then... Even then I had fantasies about it being— Well, what difference does it make now?''

"A lot to me. To use your terminology, *even then* I had my own fantasies. I allowed myself to dream that it was a ring for a real engagement. But I promise you, I would have been happy wearing a cigar band—if it came from you. Cade, I love you. And I have for a long time. I think I began to love you years ago.''

"Love is the emptiest word in the English language. It's action that puts love into force.''

"My love for you forced me not to tell you about selling out to Texas Bakeries. Sandra and Phil were planning their second honeymoon, and you had no reason to stay with me. I was afraid if I told you, you'd tell me goodbye. And I—''

He waved a hand dismissively. "Spare me.''

Her control snapped. "Spare you? Ha! You spare me, mister. How dare you march in here, holier than thou, accusing me of keeping things from you? You have a convenient memory if you've already forgotten your own lie of omission, which came to light this very evening, need I mention?''

Cade paled. They stood staring at each other, neither moving a muscle. He was the one to give. Sighing and raking a hand through his hair, he clenched his teeth. "You're right,'' he uttered, and took a step in Maureen's direction.

But she backed away from the now-extended arms that sought to pull her into an embrace.

Her action raised a look of perplexity in his face. "Look, honey, maybe I did get a little carried away. Could we..."

It was his way of apologizing, she knew. It would be so easy to accept it. Being with Cade, preferably as his wife, was what she wanted out of life, yet she forced herself to consider just what *life* meant. Day after day, year after year of dread. She refused to spend the rest of her years in the fear that she'd make a wrong move and disappoint him.

"Goodbye, Cade."

He didn't try to stop her leaving. Instead, he left her room. Left the Dry Hole. So did Maureen. Abandoning her recently purchased wardrobe, the sapphire-and-diamond ring and, of course, the unopened box he had tossed on the bed, she left the ranch. With her were her aborted hopes and broken heart.

She took an apartment, made an effort to furnish it. Days passed. Long, miserable days and nights. Had she made the right decision? she agonized over and over. Looking back on it all, though, she came to a conclusion. It was better this way.

She dropped Wilburn a note, telling him "I've moved," yet mailing it was beyond her power. He would guess that things were not well between her and Cade, and she couldn't talk about her failure.

Starting from the ground up with a new bakery didn't interest her, either, but she forced herself to the kitchen to experiment with a new line of sweets. The results tasted like cardboard.

The agony of her lonely existence was excruciating.

And then a large brown envelope arrived by registered mail. She read the cover letter; the entire contents dropped from her shaking fingers. Yet the bold scrawl of Cade's handwriting was indelibly inscribed in her brain.

This is the deed, in fee simple, to your gristmill. I'd planned to give it to you as a wedding gift—for a real partnership between the two of us. Keep it, anyway.

Cade's burnt offering rendered tears. Gallons of tears. Barrels of tears. She cried for herself and for him. For all the things that might have been. And she turned to the man who had given her comfort for a dozen years.

Two dozen days had passed since Maureen had left him. That made 576 miserable hours, 34,560 lonely minutes. Cade was a man eaten up with loss and regret.

Today was Sunday, so the Fortuna offices and PPA headquarters were closed, preventing Cade from surrounding himself with those buzzes of activity. Instead, he roamed the grounds of the Dry Hole. Ambling across his property, he stopped beside the creek and got a good look at his reflection. He looked like hell.

Pull yourself together, Herrington.

All right, he had come up with the short end of the romantic stick again, but he had to get on with his life. That was easier said than done. His far-flung business empire lacked the challenge and satisfaction of the past. Taking the helm at the PPA consumed time, but he couldn't give it the zeal it deserved. Even this ranch, this place where he had relaxed and enjoyed himself, held too many memories. Every nook and cranny, every tree and blade of grass, reminded him of Maureen.

He wasn't new to love's disappointments. His parents' divorce had wounded him, and then there had been the situation with Pam. But losing her had been child's play compared to losing Maureen.

A disobedient part of his mind drew a picture of her. As clearly as if she were standing next to him, he could picture her laughing blue eyes. He could smell the gardenia scent of her cologne. He could almost feel the warmth of her shapely body in his arms and touch the heavy fall of her sable-colored hair. And then he saw... sadness and disappointment replacing the laughter in her eyes. Had she ever cried for him?

Cade wasn't a man to cry, but he was near tears at the moment. He didn't shed a tear—he wouldn't allow himself to cry for a woman—at least on the outside. But inside... *Damn her for doing this to me.*

A march back to the house, his arms swinging at his sides, relieved not a modicum of frustration. He slammed into the house to be greeted by a scowling Frieda.

"Good gracious," she said, waving a finger at him, "you will tear the doors off the hinges if you do not settle down. And you will not settle until... If you are wanting to be happy, you should swallow your pride or whatever it is that is bothering you, and find the *Mädchen.*"

"You're not my mother, Frieda," he replied crossly.

"No, I am not." Defiant eyes drilled into him. "You know, Mr. Cade, I told the *Mädchen* about your mother. How she was sweet and kind. But I did not tell her that you remind me of Frau Herrington, when life is not going your way. Mean and sour."

"Mean and sour? Have you been hitting the schnapps?"

"I will not honor that question with a reply. But I will say this, unless you learn to trust yourself in love, you will live as she lived. Bitter till the end."

"She had good reason."

"There may be right in *reason,* but have you ever heard of forgiveness?"

Frowning, he asked, "Haven't you got something, anything, to do besides nag me?"

"I can think of something." She lifted her proud, Teutonic nose. "Find another job, if you do not quit being short with me."

Realizing that he had taken his anger out on everyone, not just his loyal housekeeper, Cade was repentant. "I'll work on my attitude, Frieda. Don't leave me. I need a semblance of order in my life."

"I won't leave you, Mr. Cade."

"Thank God."

"There is something I must tell you." Nervously, she fiddled with the silver-shot bun of hair that crowned her wide head. "There is a package for you. It arrived by delivery service. It is on your desk."

He found the box. When he'd hired the private detective to scout Maureen's new address, Cade had wanted to make amends. And now, she had responded. But how? A fist of apprehension clamped his heart as he picked up the letter that lay on top of a pile of documents.

Since you have chosen to communicate by mail, I am going along with your method. Enclosed you will find the following: a check that will retire the loan you made me; one deed to two acres of ground and a broken-down building, also known as Cutter's Mill; one legal document conveying option on same from Fortuna Enterprises and Cade Herrington to Maureen Miniver.

You will note that this box does not contain one large silver spoon. This article has been retained by the undersigned for the following reason: I feel you gave it to me with the best intentions, be it friendship or admiration or love. Forever I will cherish your gift, because it symbolizes the best part of our relationship—giving of self rather than gold.

                                                    Maureen

Cade crumbled the stilted letter. How right she was. The spoon was a small thing, but all of his pride in her accomplishments had gone into the giving. And when he added his love, he meant it. Yet he had been too distrusting to admit his feelings.

With good reason.

Yet, over the past months, he had begun to see that she was a woman beyond compare, a precious jewel that couldn't be bought. He couldn't recall a time that she wanted something material for herself, beyond Cutter's Mill.

Cutter's Mill. From the start she had been forthright about her weakness for the gristmill. Good God, he had resented her for the same thing that monopolized his being: ambition.

What a fool he was.

His ambitions had driven him to the PPA presidency. And during that quest, he had feared Maureen would discover his true motivation for the engagement scheme. Sure, she had been angry and hurt upon learning his lie of omission. But it hadn't taken long for her to forgive him.

She was the forgiving type.

But why hadn't she told him about the sale of Granny Miniver's Famous? *Use a little common sense, Herrington.* Never once had he admitted his feelings. All along, he had claimed Sandra was the pin holding the engagement together. In truth, it had been a ploy to keep Maureen at his side.

He had done more than his share of lying.

She had no reason to think he returned her love. And he yearned to tell her, "I love you." But as he had said, love was the most shallow word in the English language if it wasn't backed up by action. In his own peculiar way, he had tried to show rather than tell, but his past had held him hostage.

The past. His mean, sour, bitter past.

And the present was a jailer, too. For too long he had been driven by hate, and what had that accomplished? Financial success, personal failure.

Scrutinizing the root of his problems, Cade knew he had to settle the past if he were to have a future. The future? Hell, what about today?

What could he do today, right now, to make peace with himself? Unfortunately there was but one answer. He didn't want to do it. He had vowed never to do it. It was the last of his wishes.

But he had to make a move. And now.

Chapter Twelve

Cade's determination took him over two hundred miles west and north of San Antonio, to the town of his birth. Midland was flat, like a grade-B Western's setting, yet its industrial district was dotted with pumps resembling giant praying mantises, steel Christmas trees, drill pipes, couplings, diesel engines and huge trucks to move all of it. This was oil country. His bailiwick.

The sun beat down, baking the earth as well as Cade, while dust whirled to parch his throat. Parked in front of W. Herrington Fittings, he had yet to close the car door. His booted foot hitched on the rocker panel; his elbow rested on the cartop. He rubbed his mouth. While he needed to cure what ailed him, Cade wasn't on pins and needles to make a move toward the dilapidated, galvanized-metal warehouse. But a future with Maureen rode on whether he had the courage to take those thirty steps.

He took them.

Whistling a tune without melody over the drone of machinery, Wilburn was bent over the contraption Cade had designed. Bile rose in Cade's throat. Being in his father's presence always had that effect on him.

He started to turn, and his gaze landed on an army surplus-type desk pushed against one wall. The desk was tidy, he noted, the papers in neat stacks, the pencils all sharpened. A single yellow rose in a dime-store vase caught his attention.

Cade's line of sight moved to two framed photographs. He wasn't surprised to see that the faces of Maureen and her mother smiled from one. The other took him aback. It was a candid shot of him. Obviously it had been taken on the day he graduated from college. And the photographer? It could be none other than a person who had not been invited to the ceremony: Wilburn Herrington.

He had attended Cade's special day, had preserved the moment forever, had kept that reminder in a special place. Cade wondered how many other insights he lacked about his father.

For so many years Cade had been certain his father didn't care for him. Of course, there had been the overtures of reconciliation, but he had always assumed greed was the motivation, that Wilburn wanted to share in the Fortuna wealth.

He glanced at the man who was hard at work, making his own fortune. *Since I was wrong about Maureen, could I be wrong about my father?*

But his resentment was a long-term part of his being, and Cade refused to weaken.

Cade walked toward him. "We need to talk."

A smile lit the old man's tired eyes, then his expression turned guarded. After wiping his hands on a faded red rag, Wilburn put the cloth aside. "What can I do for you, son?"

"Would a cup of coffee and a few minutes of your time be asking too much?"

A grin softened Wilburn's lined features. "Just made a pot. And time? You got it. Have a seat, son." He busied himself pouring two mugs of steaming coffee, then handed the more presentable of the chipped vessels to his son. Settled in a gun-metal gray chair that somewhat matched the one Cade took, Wilburn sipped the mud-thick brew. "I reckon you're here to see how everything's progressing with the couplings re-rounder. It's a beauty, and I'm wondering if you're willing to sell me the patent. I—"

"You've done a good job, but I'm not here about the machine. This visit has to do with you and me. And Maureen." Cade cupped his suddenly chilled hands around the mug. "A good while back, I promised her I'd spend some time with you, but I suppose you know all about that."

Wilburn nodded.

"I never intended to keep my promise."

"Wouldn't take a genius to figure that out, son. But you're here now. Which counts for something."

Cade put the cup on the desk, stood and began to pace the concrete floor. Shoving the tips of his fingers into the back pockets of his jeans, he glanced at the ceiling, then downward before stopping to turn troubled eyes to his father. "I've hated you for a long time. Do you want to know why?"

"I have a fair idea. It's over your mother."

"You got it." Cade clenched his teeth. "It takes a rotten man to do what you did."

"You're right," Wilburn replied and paled. "I was a lousy husband and father."

"But it appears you were sterling in that department when it came to Maureen and her mother."

"They were my second chance."

"Why didn't you give *my* mother a chance?"

"Son, if I could do things differently, I'd do them. A body can't go back, though. All I can do is learn from it and try to do better, now and in the future. But I want you to know—your mother was a fine woman and I always admired her."

As Wilburn had said, nothing could be done about the past. Except try to understand it, try to learn from it. Cade had learned from the past, yet he took the wrong lessons.

Cade thought about what Frieda had said about his mother. Yes, that fine woman had gone unhappy and unforgiving to her grave. He didn't want to make the same mistake, so he had to find the truth.

"Why did you tomcat around on her?" he asked.

Wilburn studied his cup.

Assuming he'd get no reply from the man who had kept a closed mouth for two decades, Cade exhaled and changed the subject. "I suppose you know Maureen and I have split."

"I do." Wilburn's voice was barely above a whisper. "And it hurts me. I was certain you two were meant for each other. That's why I went along with her harebrained scheme to begin with. So the two of you would have time to get to know each other."

"You mean you had some sort of matchmaking in mind?"

"Not exactly, but I did have a few thoughts along that line."

"Why?"

"Because I wanted my two kids to find what they were lacking in life. I wanted Maureen to be with a fellow who'd keep her on her toes and her mind off that cookie factory. As for you . . . well, son, you need a good woman like Maureen."

Cade needed her in the worst way.

"Never asked nobody for nothing, not my baby girl," Wilburn was saying. "All she wanted was to make something of herself." He took a sip of coffee. "Bless her heart, she started with nothing but a few cookie sheets and a dream to succeed, and she made something of herself. All she lacked was the human things. Someone to love and be loved by. Course, she had my love, but that's not the same as having a sweetheart."

"Cut the sales pitch."

"I would, but there's too much at stake here. You don't know how hard it's been these last days, my wanting to storm into your office and pound some sense into your head. But I didn't do it, because she begged me not to. That girl's got a lot of pride." Wilburn clamped Cade's shoulder. "She made a mistake, not telling you about selling out to Texas Bakeries, but who doesn't make mistakes? I made a ton of them with you and your mama. I'm guilty of everything charged against me. But, Lord, boy, I've regretted every one of those foolish things. Dumb mistakes are easy to do and hard to rectify."

Cade considered those frank words. Somehow, he didn't doubt Wilburn's honesty. His admiration for his father grew. It took a lot of guts, owning up to sins.

"I'm an old man," Wilburn went on. "Maybe I've got ten years, maybe one. What will I go to my grave with? Guilt. And shame at losing out all those years with you."

"What about Mom? Did you ever love her?"

"Son, when Rowena and I started out, she was like the fireworks at New Year's. Bright, shining and exhilarating. And I think I was that to her, too."

Fireworks. There were no fireworks in Cade's empty life without Maureen.

"We burned ourselves out," Wilburn was saying, "expecting too much out of each other."

I've been guilty of that, too. And Cade thought about his mother. Though he had loved her unequivocably, had been her ally against his father, Cade admitted inwardly that she hadn't been perfect. She had expected the world to fall at her feet. And when it didn't, she had fallen apart. She, too, had made mistakes.

Glancing at the rosebud, Cade asked, "Are you the one who sends birthday roses to her grave?"

"She always appreciated a yellow rose." Wilburn's look was abashed. "It's the little things that are important."

A rose was something like a silver spoon. Of all the things Cade had done for Maureen, the measly spoon was the most cherished. The one she had kept.

"I wish we'd had this talk a long time ago," Cade admitted.

"Better late than never, son."

Cade cut his eyes to the photographs, to the yellow rose. "What's the flower for?"

"To remind me of the good times with your mama."

The good times. Cade recalled many of them, recollections he had pushed from his thoughts for many years. His parents laughing and joking, kissing and hugging. And then came the bad times. Their estrangement, then the divorce settlement that his father had demanded. But he had to quit thinking along that line.

Maybe the old man had figured he had it coming, since he was the one who made the money for Pemberton Couplings. Money, be damned.

It was in the past, and Wilburn obviously had some lingering feelings for the first Mrs. Herrington. Maybe this was all Cade wanted to know. That his father wasn't the bastard of his long-held beliefs. Sure, he had his faults. Who didn't?

Suddenly, Cade ached for all the years they had lost.

"Pop," he said, using the word for the first time in two decades, "do you think there's a chance you and I could start over again? And make it better this time?"

"Absolutely."

It was as if Cade's spirit were washed, leaving him clean and invigorated for life. But not quite.

"Do you think Maureen will take me back?" he asked his father.

"She's a forgiving gal, you know. Mighty forgiving."

"How . . . how is she, Pop?"

"Miserable. She's lost interest in everything. All she does is cry over you."

It was wicked, Cade's satisfaction that she cared enough to cry over him, yet his chest clamped as he considered her misery. "Pop, what are you doing for the next couple of days?"

"I was planning to work, but if you've got a better idea, I'm game."

"Yeah, I've got a better idea."

Night had fallen. Maureen's sparsely furnished and dimly lit apartment was quiet as a tomb. It might as well have been a crypt; she felt only half alive. The clock that sat on a TV tray read nine o'clock.

Another day without Cade. She needed to accept her pain and get on with the business of living, but the days weren't getting any easier. What had these lonely hours been like for Cade? She didn't doubt he was suffering. He'd had a lifetime of it.

Tears welled for him.

But even if he walked through her door right now, declaring love and undying devotion, she couldn't grant him free license over her heart. She wouldn't live in fear of wronging and disappointing.

A knock at her front door pulled her to her feet. When she opened the door, she faced the object of her considerations.

Joy and apprehension, love and uncertainty—these emotions shot through her as she eyed Cade.

"What brings you here?" she asked hesitantly.

"You." He took a step toward her. "I have something to tell you. I love you." He bent on one knee and took her hand. "Tomorrow is the first of October. The anniversary of my first gusher. I believe that's the day everyone is expecting us to marry."

"I'm sure you've put your friends straight."

"No, I haven't. Because I'm hoping we'll be saying 'I do' tomorrow." He smiled and it had sexy written all over it. "I've missed you. Tell me you missed me."

She yearned to, but unless Cade had made peace with his father, he was still the same man, and she doubted anything had happened between the two Herringtons. "You miss the itch when you get rid of it."

He chuckled. "Maybe that's why I've been missing you. You're an itch I can't scratch."

"Try calamine lotion."

"I don't want to get rid of the itch I have for you."

"Sure. Until I do something to displease you. Something like, act as if I'm a human being with normal weaknesses."

"Yes, I was angry at you, but you've been mad at me, too," he pointed out. "Doesn't mean we can't get glad just like we got mad."

"Since you're in a forgiving frame of mind, you ought to give your father a break."

Cade grinned. "Looks like the odds have turned in my favor." He strode over to the window, pushed up the sash and yelled to the street, "Hey, Pop, look alive! Get in here on the double."

"Wilburn is with you?" she asked incredulously.

"That's right. Pop and I are here to change your mind about becoming Mrs. Cade Herrington. Matter of fact, he's going to be my best man."

"You're joking."

"Not on your life." Cade grabbed her into his arms, twirling her around and around. He stopped to give her a deep and delicious kiss. "Will you, or will you not, run off to some seedy marriage mill in Nuevo Laredo and become my wife? Will you promise to retire to some equally ratty motel room and allow me to show you how much I adore you?"

Oh my, his words were wonderful!

"Douglas will say that's socially unacceptable. And your friends will be disappointed if we don't invite them to the wedding."

Cade nuzzled her neck and received the proper response. Pleased, he replied, "We'll throw a reception when we get back from Switzerland. But if you'd prefer a proper wedding, all show and white lace, I'm all for it. Provided we can get it arranged by tomorrow. I've waited long enough for you."

"I don't need fancy trappings. But aren't we being a bit hasty about all this?"

"My darling, blue-eyed sweetheart, we've been engaged for weeks. There's nothing hasty about the wedding."

She heard the front door open. From the corner of her eye, she spied a beaming Wilburn Herrington. She winked at him, then grinned up at Cade. "What does Dad think about all this?" she asked unnecessarily.

"I say—*it's about time!* Now come on, kiddos, quit arguing about this, that or the other. Make your ole papa happy. Cade, give her another kiss. Maureen, get packed. Let's get this show on the road!"

They did.

*   *   *   *   *

Silhouette Romance®

LONG, TALL TEXANS

HARDEN
Diana Palmer

In her bestselling LONG, TALL TEXANS series, Diana Palmer brought you to Jacobsville and introduced you to the rough and rugged ranchers who call the town home. Now, hot and dusty Jacobsville promises to get even hotter when hard-hearted, woman-hating rancher Harden Tremayne has to reckon with the lovely Miranda Warren.

The LONG, TALL TEXANS series continues! Don't miss HARDEN by Diana Palmer in March . . . only from Silhouette Romance.

LTT-1

WRITTEN IN THE STARS

Will The Pisces Man Be Lured Into Romance?

Find out in March with FOR HEAVEN'S SAKE by Brenda Trent . . . the third book in our WRITTEN IN THE STARS series!

There was only one fish in the sea for pet groomer Kelly-Ann Keernan—she'd fallen for sexy Steve Jamison, hook, line and sinker! But will the private Pisces man ever say goodbye to bachelorhood and hello to married bliss?

Be sure to catch the passionate Pisces man's story, FOR HEAVEN'S SAKE by Brenda Trent . . . only from Silhouette Romance!

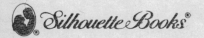
Silhouette Books®

SILHOUETTE'S "BIG WIN"
SWEEPSTAKES RULES & REGULATIONS
NO PURCHASE NECESSARY TO ENTER OR RECEIVE A PRIZE

1. To enter the Sweepstakes and join the Reader Service, scratch off the metallic strips on all your BIG WIN tickets #1-#6. This will reveal the potential values for each Sweepstakes entry number, the number of free book(s) you will receive and your free bonus gift as part of our Reader Service. If you do not wish to take advantage of our Reader Service but wish to enter the Sweepstakes only, scratch off the metallic strips on your BIG WIN tickets #1-#4. Return your entire sheet of tickets intact. Incomplete and/or inaccurate entries are ineligible for that section or sections of prizes. Torstar Corp. and its affiliates are not responsible for mutilated or unreadable entries or inadvertent printing errors. Mechanically reproduced entries are null and void.

2. Whether you take advantage of this offer or not, on or about April 30, 1992, at the offices of Marden-Kane Inc., Lake Success, NY, your Sweepstakes numbers will be compared against the list of winning numbers generated at random by the computer. However, prizes will only be awarded to individuals who have entered the Sweepstakes. In the event that all prizes are not claimed, a random drawing will be held from all qualified entries received from March 30, 1990 to March 31, 1992, to award all unclaimed prizes. All cash prizes (Grand to Sixth), will be mailed to the winners and are payable by check in U.S. funds. Seventh prize will be shipped to winners via third-class mail. These prizes are in addition to any free, surprise or mystery gifts that might be offered. Versions of this Sweepstakes with different prizes of approximate equal value may appear at retail outlets or in other mailings by Torstar Corp. and its affiliates.

3. The following prizes are awarded in this sweepstakes: ★ Grand Prize (1) $1,000,000; First Prize (1) $25,000; Second Prize (1) $10,000; Third Prize (5) $5,000; Fourth Prize (10) $1,000; Fifth Prize (100) $250; Sixth Prize (2,500) $10; ★ ★ Seventh Prize (6,000) $12.95 ARV.

   ★ This presentation offers a Grand Prize of a $1,000,000 annuity. Winner will receive $33,333.33 a year for 30 years without interest totalling $1,000,000.

   ★ ★ Seventh Prize: A fully illustrated hardcover book published by Torstar Corp. Approximate Retail Value of the book is $12.95.

   Entrants may cancel the Reader Service at anytime without cost or obligation to buy (see details in center insert card).

4. This Sweepstakes is being conducted under the supervision of an independent judging organization. By entering this Sweepstakes, each entrant accepts and agrees to be bound by these rules and the decisions of the judges, which shall be final and binding. Odds of winning in the random drawing are dependent upon the total number of entries received. Taxes, if any, are the sole responsibility of the winners. Prizes are nontransferable. All entries must be received at the address printed on the reply card and must be postmarked no later than 12:00 MIDNIGHT on March 31, 1992. The drawing for all unclaimed Sweepstakes prizes will take place on May 30, 1992, at 12:00 NOON, at the offices of Marden-Kane, Inc., Lake Success, New York.

5. This offer is open to residents of the U.S., the United Kingdom, France and Canada, 18 years or older, except employees and their immediate family members of Torstar Corp., its affiliates, subsidiaries, and all the other agencies, entities and persons connected with the use, marketing or conduct of this Sweepstakes. All Federal, State, Provincial and local laws apply. Void wherever prohibited or restricted by law. Any litigation within the Province of Quebec respecting the conduct and awarding of a prize in this publicity contest must be submitted to the Régie des Loteries et Courses du Québec.

6. Winners will be notified by mail and may be required to execute an affidavit of eligibility and release, which must be returned within 14 days after notification or an alternate winner will be selected. Canadian winners will be required to correctly answer an arithmetical skill-testing question administered by mail, which must be returned within a limited time. Winners consent to the use of their names, photographs and/or likenesses for advertising and publicity in conjunction with this and similar promotions without additional compensation. For a list of our major prize winners, send a stamped, self-addressed ENVELOPE to: WINNERS LIST, c/o Marden-Kane Inc., P.O. Box 701, SAYREVILLE, NJ 08871. Requests for Winners Lists will be fulfilled after the May 30, 1992 drawing date.

If Sweepstakes entry form is missing, please print your name and address on a 3″ ×5″ piece of plain paper and send to:

In the U.S.
Silhouette's "BIG WIN" Sweepstakes
3010 Walden Ave.
P.O. Box 1867
Buffalo, NY 14269-1867

In Canada
Silhouette's "BIG WIN" Sweepstakes
P.O. Box 609
Fort Erie, Ontario
L2A 5X3

Offer limited to one per household.

© 1991 Harlequin Enterprises Limited   Printed in the U.S.A.

LTY-S391D

SILHOUETTE·INTIMATE·MOMENTS®

NORA ROBERTS
Night Shadow

People all over the city of Urbana were asking, Who was that masked man?

Assistant district attorney Deborah O'Roarke was the first to learn his secret identity . . . and her life would never be the same.

The stories of the lives and loves of the O'Roarke sisters began in January 1991 with NIGHT SHIFT, Silhouette Intimate Moments #365. And if you want to know more about Deborah and the man behind the mask, look for NIGHT SHADOW, Silhouette Intimate Moments #373.

Available now at your favorite retail outlet, or order your copy by sending your name, address, zip or postal code along with a check or money order for $2.95 (please do not send cash), plus 75¢ postage and handling, payable to Silhouette Reader Service to:

In the U.S.	In Canada
3010 Walden Ave.	P.O. Box 609
P.O. Box 1396	Fort Erie, Ontario
Buffalo, NY 14269-1396	L2A 5X3

Please specify book title(s) with your order.
Canadian residents add applicable federal and provincial taxes.

NITE-1A

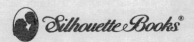
Silhouette Books®